Rusty P

THE DRUG TASK FORCE

The Cartel

Thank you for your support and hope you enjoy it

Rusty

outskirtspress
DENVER, COLORADO

This is a work of fiction. The events and characters described herein are imaginary and are not intended to refer to specific places or living persons. The opinions expressed in this manuscript are solely the opinions of the author and do not represent the opinions or thoughts of the publisher. The author has represented and warranted full ownership and/ or legal right to publish all the materials in this book.

The Drug Task Force
The Cartel
All Rights Reserved.
Copyright © 2013 Rusty Pope
v2.0

Cover Photo © 2013 Greg Merrell and JupiterImages Corporation. All rights reserved - used with permission.

This book may not be reproduced, transmitted, or stored in whole or in part by any means, including graphic, electronic, or mechanical without the express written consent of the publisher except in the case of brief quotations embodied in critical articles and reviews.

Outskirts Press, Inc.
http://www.outskirtspress.com

ISBN: 978-1-4787-1320-3

Outskirts Press and the "OP" logo are trademarks belonging to Outskirts Press, Inc.

PRINTED IN THE UNITED STATES OF AMERICA

Chapter 1

Pablo slipped into his old, comfortable black leather Justin boots, kissed his wife, Karen, while she slept, and then headed for the door.

Karen rolled over and whispered, "Not again."

He knew he had a job to do, though, and this time he could tell it was something very big. The damp, low clouds and fog mirrored his heavy mood as he maneuvered his undercover truck through the inky black streets toward Nightmare Alley. The truck had been recently seized in a drug raid, and except for the bullet holes in the left quarter panel and the leather of the passenger seat, it was like new. Pablo spoke on his cell phone with Corporal Tommy Hamms, while Chance Roman was trying to set up a meeting with a C.I., confidential informant. Margaret, a Hispanic female with long dark brown hair, had called Pablo earlier in the day and explained something about a major marijuana drug shipment.

The phone calls from other women were driving a wedge between Pablo and Karen and his grandfatherly duties. Pablo was trying to keep a balance in his life but was sliding down a slippery slope into the drug world and culture. Karen had been his anchor during thirty-one years of unwavering marriage, but he could sense that she was losing patience with him. Pablo was actually a Chickasaw-Choctaw American with a given name of Sonny Smoke, but he received the nickname of Pablo just two days after joining the Tulsa County Drug Task Force. His dark complexion and long dark hair often caused him to be mistaken for being of Hispanic ethnicity, so Sonny had become Pablo.

Pablo turned toward the darkest part of any town, a dead-end street that prostitutes, dealers, and gang members called home, a dead end for all hopes and dreams. He'd been there at least a dozen times before for arrests, murders, and drugs, but this time he came for information, although he did not yet realize the danger of it.

Corporal Hamms and Roman, in their undercover trucks, were in position to cover and record the conversation between Pablo and Margaret. He searched the alley for her. From the tinted window of his comfortable perch, he barely spied her. She stood scarcely noticeable, crouched behind a dumpster under an eave that was dimly lit with one street lamp. Pablo parked in the darkness and stepped cautiously toward the back of the alley to ensure she was alone.

Yes, she was alone. She was a thin waif of a woman. That night, her long, thinning brown hair looked more like an old feather duster, and her skin twitched

THE DRUG TASK FORCE

as he approached her. She looked even more desperate than he had remembered. Just two years earlier, she had been a young trophy wife full of life, until she was introduced to methamphetamine, or "ice." Her methamphetamine habit had consumed her. Her once-beautiful brown eyes faded into the dark circles of her sullen face, and the track marks on her arms could guide a freight train to hell and back.

Pablo reached into his pocket and plucked a damp $100 bill for her. Margaret shook nearly uncontrollably as she snatched the cash from his hand and slipped it beneath her tattered black leather-and-lace bra. No doubt the money would buy her some comfort either in a liquid or powder form, he thought, yet he needed her. He needed the tip that only a confidential informant like Margaret could deliver, so the devil pact between an addict and an officer sworn to stop drugs was sealed. With her information, twenty-four hours of purgatory would begin.

Pablo stepped outside his house at 0710 hours on a chilled and cloudy October morning after he has kissed Karen good-bye for the second time in the past few hours. From her passive response, Pablo sensed that she was annoyed that he continued to carry his work home. It was Monday, and after a hard weekend of watching football and beer, Pablo was headed to work. He wore cargo pants, a brown work shirt with a Natural Gas logo, and tennis shoes in case of a foot pursuit with the Mexicans, and his favorite ball cap. Pablo just loved his new work uniform. Pablo, a veteran officer of twenty years with the Sand Springs Police Department, headed to the drug task force office. He had craved a new career opportunity when he signed up for the task force three years earlier.

That morning, as usual, Pablo honked and swore in a wretched traffic jam as Chance Roman called him on the radio. "Pablo, hey buddy, you on the radio?"

"What now, Roman?" Pablo answered.

"I need some help watching the house," Roman pleaded.

"Give me an address and directions. This time good directions, though," Pablo answered with hope that this time his team would not try to get him lost. He grimaced, though, as he thought of his team members always trying to get him, the small-town cop, lost in the big city.

"Two three one oh North McKinley, second house with a red truck. We are goin' to bust the weed dealers today, boys," Roman announced over the radio to all who were listening.

"Is this our house from last night's information?" Pablo asked.

"Yeah, it is, and it's a good one," Roman proudly answered.

THE DRUG TASK FORCE

"This is a nice neighborhood on North McKinley," Lowery pitched in.

"I'm about ten minutes out, if I can squeeze out of this traffic jam and get by this dang ol' grandma," Pablo answered with frustration in his voice.

Pablo drove past the target house and circled back around. It was in a nice middle-class neighborhood, a red brick house with a manicured front yard and a red 2010 Chevy truck with something in Spanish printed on the tinted back window. The house was the second one on the west side of the street, with no other cars in the driveway.

"Roman, I guess we're watchin' Mexicans this morning," Lowery commented.

"Rich Mexicans," Roman answered. "Pablo's informant saw 200 pounds of weed in the garage, and I typed the warrant last night."

Roman asked, "Can you guys sit on this till I get the warrant signed?" He added with a smile in his voice, "Pablo, after you met with the informant and got the address, I came over and sat on the house for a few hours, and the traffic was heavier than Walmart."

Pablo replied, "This is so great; I knew she had the right information. Almost makes me proud of her. But make sure you're back here before I run out of coffee." Pablo laughed.

"I'm here, where do you want me?" Lowery loudly asked.

RUSTY POPE

"Don't park in the target's driveway like last time," Pablo smarted off.

Mike Lowery, a younger officer, had been with the D.T.F. for one and a half years, Pablo three years, and Freddy Humphries one year. All three officers were from different agencies. Chance Roman, Corporal Tommy Hamms, and Sergeant Robert Davis were from the host agency, the Tulsa County sheriff's office, also Joey Brown, who just returned to duty after a broken-hand incident.

The neighborhood was a typical middle-class neighborhood with tree-lined streets, decent cars, and children's toys in most of the front yards. The target house was a single-story red-brick home with a two-car garage and a privacy fence around the back. The front of the house had a deep, dark, narrow entryway with a barred security storm door and a decorative front wooden door. Roman called everyone on the radio to meet, brief, and suit up for the search warrant.

"I am already suited up; I will stay here with eyes on the house," Humphries announced.

"Let's meet at the Warehouse Market on Lincoln around back. We can brief and suit up there," Hamms ordered.

"They better have coffee and cigarettes; only three left," Pablo stated.

All team members were arriving on the back side

THE DRUG TASK FORCE

of the supermarket with Pablo, in his green GMC truck, a Mexican hoopty. Lowery had a black tinted-out BMW. Roman had a gray Chevy work truck. Hamms drove a pretty fancy silver truck. Brown had a brown extended-cab Chevy truck, with Sergeant Davis in a pimped-out black Dodge truck. Also arriving was Corporal Warren Organ, who was the uniformed deputy they used for search warrants. Also two reserve deputies, Johnny Walker and Randy Hawk, were there. Roman began the briefing and giving out assignments.

"Bad guys are Hispanic, and they have connections with mid-level weed suppliers. They can and have had several hundred pounds of weed at this location. This target house is a prime location for this supply route. Informant says they have straight connections with Mexico and they deal all over this area. There are three Hispanic males, Eduardo Warez, Jamie Esponza, and Ricco Campo, and all three are illegal and have been arrested several times for drugs. They all have weapons charges in their history. C.I. said they saw about two hundred pounds last night in six duffle bags in the garage. Boys, I am telling you these are real bad guys, so get your game faces on," Roman instructed.

Hamms began and gave out the assignments. "Organ, knock and announce. Lowery, Pablo, and then Brown, with the ram. Roman is team leader, Humpme, then me and Davis. Walker and Hawk, you guys got the back. Once the door is breached, call all suspects out, and then we enter. Remember, if shots are fired and one of us gets injured, the next two step over and engage, and the rest will pull the injured out and we make it an armed and barricaded situation. Our injured go to St. Michael's Hospital, and the bad guys go to Hilltop. Go slow, identify, and don't miss," Hamms ordered.

"Boys, a pimped-out blue Dodge truck just arrived, and two Hispanic males are getting out and entering the target house. I cannot see the tag, but they are carrying in something in a black nylon sport bag," Humphries radioed in.

Pablo, who wore brown cargo jeans and tennis shoes, pulled off his work shirt and changed into his raid jersey over his bulletproof vest. Lowery wore blue jeans and a vest with black jersey and a drop-down holster. Hamms had 511 jeans, vest, jersey, and duty holster and carried a FN 303 pepper paintball gun. Brown had jeans, jersey with an FBI. vest, and a drop-down holster and carried an "ump" 223. Humphries had jeans, vest, jersey, and duty holster and carried the less-lethal shotgun. Roman, with a vest, jersey, and duty holsters, carried another "ump" 223. All team members carried a Glock 40 as the primary duty weapon.

As everyone was loading up, Pablo yelled out.

"The truck is leaving with Hispanic males, and not

THE DRUG TASK FORCE

the same ones that just got here." Humphries again on the radio.

"How about this for a game face?" Pablo said with a big smile. Pablo had put some black shoe polish under his eyes like the eye black that athletes wear on game days. All chuckled, but they were clearly gearing up for serious business. While in route to the target house, team members talked to each other on the private secure channel on the police radio.

"Sergeant, can you put us out ten-ninety-seven when we get close?" questioned Hamms.

"Ten-four," answered Sergeant Roberts.

"Humpme, you still have your mustache?" Lowery said jokingly.

"Yes, but it is not as dark as it was yesterday," answered Humphries.

"Did you guys hear Rush Limbaugh call the president an economic jackass on national radio?" Pablo said with a laugh.

As the guys were at Hamms's house watching college football Saturday night, Humphries was the first to pass out and therefore receive the Magic Marker mustache, a typical Saturday night the boys like and wives and girlfriends hate. Just about every Monday morning, someone had a Magic Marker disguise. Only once had a wife or girlfriend received the trophy; the boys were grounded for a week.

RUSTY POPE

"I think it makes you look older and smarter," Brown stated

"I don't need the older, maybe smarter, though," replied Humphries.

"Let's take up both sides of the street when we park. Nobody needs to get through, anyway," broadcasted Hamms.

Roman led the parade and stopped one house short of the target house, and then Walker and Hawk continued to drive over one more block and drive through the alley to get to the back of the house. Hawk and Walker were the two oldest members of the team and always covered the back during search warrants. Johnny Walker, a retired fireman, was the oldest of the team, but by no means a weak link. Walker could shoot well enough with his less-than-lethal shotgun, but he could not hear very well. This time a privacy fence added a degree of difficulty to their assignment. The team lined up and started their approach. Walker was on the radio.

"Three mean ass pit bulls back here and they are not chained up." stated Walker.

Barking came from the back yard, a lot of angry barking. Hawk and Walker were armed with their duty Glocks, Walker with the high-powered F.N. 303 pepper paintball gun, and Hawk, who traded with Humphries, had the less-lethal 12-gauge shotgun. As the team made its approach and as Organ was knocking, screams, shotgun blasts, and paintball guns fired. The two reserve deputies entered the yard through the back gate and were attacked by three angry pit bulls. Also one Hispanic male had come out of the back garage door and opened fire on them. The two men split off in different areas of the back yard and tried to reach cover from the bullets and teeth.

"Shoot that son of a bitch, Hawk; move, get down," screamed Walker.

More gunfire came from the back yard, and Davis and Hamms broke the line and started to go around back.

"No, no, stop! Cross-fire. Brown, get that damn door open!" yelled Hamms.

For only the second time ever, Brown broke open the door with one hit, and as the front door flew open, Walker and Hawk were in a fierce gun battle in the back yard. The two reserve deputies were out-gunned and out-manned, counting the three pit bulls. Hawk, during the first blast, took two hits, one in the leg and one in the shoulder but managed to crawl to the back side of a metal shed. Walker had engaged two of the pit bulls and killed one and seriously wounded the other. Walker managed to get to his Glock as he emptied his ten-shot pepper ball gun. Hawk returned fire toward the bad guy and gave Walker a chance to get to cover behind a big oak tree. As Hawk was reaching for his Glock, a pit found him and bit and clawed at Hawk's wounded leg. Walker became engaged with the bad guy, who had run out of ammunition for his assault rifle and was using a handgun. The Hispanic male was in full attack mode and was circling the yard and got a clean shot at Walker. Walker, trying to see around the tree, did not notice him quickly enough and took two rounds. Walker fell but did not go without hitting the man once.

Hawk was still engaged with the pit when he noticed Walker falling to the ground. During his struggle with the pit, Hawk was able to get a shot off at the pit as it was eating his leg. Hawk turned back to where Walker had just fallen, but the bad guy arrived and shot him three times in the chest with a reloaded assault rifle.

As the battle was raging out back, the entry team was making entry, with fingers on the trigger. The front door open, the team could see straight into the living room and could also see the back yard through the sliding glass door.

With no need to announce who they were, the team made entry with Organ leading them in, and they went straight in and then held the corner of the living room and hallway. The living room had just a couple of pieces of furniture, more like outside furniture,

THE DRUG TASK FORCE

a plastic table and several plastic chairs, a big screen television, and one sofa along the far wall. On the tabletop were three glass bongs for smoking marijuana, several empty beer cans, and chips spilled out everywhere. All dopers seem to have big screens and all the latest video games.

The kitchen had only a fridge and microwave oven and just a few other items on the countertop. The house was just a doper's flop house for storing and selling dope.

With Organ, Pablo, and Lowery holding the hallway, Hamms, Brown, and Roman circled the room and entered the kitchen area and cleared it. They then entered the garage, and all they found was a real nicely cleaned garage with six duffle bags lined up in the middle of the floor. They then shouted "Clear" to let the others know they were secure. They rejoined the line and covered for Organ, Pablo, and Lowery to take the hall, bedrooms, and bathroom.

Organ said, "Hold that door." It was closed and no threat to the team. As Organ turned back to the first bedroom with Lowery, the door came open, and all they saw was a muzzle flash and the loud sound of a shotgun. Organ took the hit in the chest and fell back in the hallway floor. Lowery and Pablo then got on target, even before the man could pump the shotgun to reload. Pablo and Lowery, each with a double tap, shot the man in the chest and then stepped over Organ the secure the man and the room. Hamms, Roman, and Brown then took the bathroom and started to enter the last bedroom, when they heard the window break. They readied themselves for an armed suspect entry and opened the door.

Brown went first, and he noticed that the window was open and caught a glimpse of a male running through the back yard toward the privacy fence. They still had to clear the bedroom, and it was secured in a few seconds. Brown then looked back to the fence and did not see any suspects in the back yard. Sergeant Davis, having been outside the whole time, worked his way around to the back yard and caught a glimpse of the bad guys diving into a brown older-model Ford truck that was parked in the alley. Sergeant Davis did manage to fire off four rounds at the truck tailgate as the truck sped away through the alley. Sergeant Davis did see and remember the truck tag, OK-713-FMG. "Dispatch, check OK tag 713-FMG, and where the hell is my ambulance?" yelled Sergeant Davis.

As the battles were raging inside and out, Sergeant Davis was on the radio calling for more backup and ambulances. Soon the air was filled with the sounds of sirens and radio traffic. Brown and Lowery stayed with Organ while Pablo and the others went out back to check on the two fallen deputies. Organ took his hit in the chest, which was lucky, since he had worn his bulletproof vest. In the back, Hawk was not as lucky. His leg was half eaten off, and the dead pit bull still had its jaws clenched on Hawk's leg. The three rounds he suffered were from the assault rifle, and his vest did little to protect him from the onslaught of the .223 ammo. Hawk was pronounced dead at the scene.

When Pablo got to Walker, he still had a pulse. Walker's wounds were to his upper left shoulder and to his gut just under his vest. Walker was shot with a nine millimeter handgun the bad guy had used when he ran out of ammo and before he reloaded. Pablo stayed with Walker until the medics arrived, and even then, they had to make Pablo leave. Pablo walked with the medics as they carried Walker on the gurney to the ambulance. He helped load his friend into the back of the ambulance. "Hang in there, you old no-hearing pain in my ass, man," whispered Pablo.

No more words were spoken, just silent disbelief as to what had just taken place. Team members were covered in blood, sweat, and some tears as the ambulances loaded up their fallen friends and sped off to the hospital.

Chapter 2

TIME IS 10:20 HRS.

Back inside the house, still no one wanted to speak, as if this whole incident had not really happened.

Hamms then looked at Roman as the team had gathered in the living room. "What in the hell just happened here? Tell me what the hell happened," Hamms pleaded.

"I don't know; I just don't know," Roman answered.

"It was like they were ready for us an ambush maybe," Brown said.

"The pits bulls on guard in the back with one bad guy and one each in both of the bedrooms just waiting for us to enter the hallway," Humphries offered.

"Yes, like a fucking ambush. I tell you they were ready for us," Lowery stated.

Pablo came in from the garage. "Boys, we are at war, and they just signed their death wish, or ours. Come out here in the garage and get ready for this shit," Pablo said with pain in his voice.

As the other five team members joined Pablo in the garage and saw a very clean garage with nothing parked or piled up in the middle of the floor and nothing on the freshly painted walls. It looked like a brand-new garage. The only items in the entire garage were six military-style duffle bags placed neatly in the middle of the floor. On each of the duffle bags was three-inch masking tape with one word, the name of a team member, as if the bags actually belonged to each one of them. They quickly but safely went to their bag. Each was flat but for Pablo's, which looked like it had a basketball inside. The others watched as Pablo picked up his bag, which was wet and heavy. He tilted the bag forward, and blood started dripping out. A ball followed; not a basketball, but a severed head fell to the ground and rolled. Pablo, fearing the worst, fell to his knees and stopped the head from rolling. The head had short, dirty-blond hair, the color of Pablo's wife's hair. Pablo quickly picked up the head and then realized that it was not his wife, but the head did belong to someone he knew. It was the head of the informant, Margaret, who had furnished the information to Pablo, Roman, and Hamms about this house.

"What the hell is this? Oh shit! It's Margaret!" screamed Pablo.

"Damn it, Pablo how could this have happened?" Roman said with disbelief.

"Oh my god, how could they have found out about her?" Hamms said as he kicked the garage door.

"I don't know, but look in your bags, man; we have got us some real fucking problems now," explained Lowery.

RUSTY POPE

Pablo stepped back for a few seconds to remember when he and Roman had first met up with Margaret. A simple marijuana bust of her and her rich husband, and they warned her then about the road she was taking and then the second time, when they put her husband away for forty years for trafficking meth or ice. He knew then that she was not the same person, for the ice addiction had already taken a hold of her, and now this.

"All right, boys, this is personal now, and damn it, she did not deserve this. Someone has to pay for this," Pablo exclaimed.

Pablo's bag also had a picture of his wife, three grandchildren, and his house on the lake. Lowery's bag had a picture of his girlfriend, home. Brown's bag had his wife and home. Hamms's bag had his wife, home and their two dogs. Roman's bag also had pictures of his wife, two children, and their home as well. After a few minutes of everyone feeling gut kicked, the cold chills subsided.

Pablo broke the silence. "Told you guys we are now at war, and we aren't taking any prisoners," roared Pablo.

"Fucking A, and this time no one is going to jail tonight," Brown stated harshly.

Sergeant Davis, seeing all this for the first time, got on the radio and ordered deputies to get to the homes

THE DRUG TASK FORCE

of all the deputies on the task force. He also gave orders not to let anyone in or around the homes. Pablo got on his cell phone and called his police department and had someone go to his house and keep an eye on it until he got there. He then called his wife and told her to meet him at a location right then. Lowery and Humphries did the same with their own agencies.

Chapter 3

As the team members left the North McKinley address, they were all filled with anger, remorse, disbelief, dread, and a since of uncertainty as to their own futures. They were not scared for their own protection, but scared for the safety of their families and the families of their friends. One word to describe what was raging in their hearts was redemption, redemption for the ambush, redemption for the injuries sustained by Organ and Walker, and redemption for the murder of Hawk. As they were leaving the scene, there was an update put out over the radio about the status of the two injured deputies. Organ is okay and would remain in the hospital until the next day. Walker was in surgery and the odds were not good that a man of his age would survive.

Pablo took the assault on Walker very hard, not only because a deputy was shot in the line of duty, but also the two had become close friends. Pablo took Walker under his wing and helped to train Walker, more or less. Pablo was always yelling, "Damn it, Walker." He teased Walker of being deaf, blind, and having Alzheimer's disease, but most of all, Pablo and Walker were the only smokers. After search warrants,

THE DRUG TASK FORCE

the two would wind up smoking cigarettes and drinking coffee. Rumor had it that Walker, covering the back, stopped a fleeing suspect with his less-lethal shotgun while smoking with one hand and holding a coffee cup in the other. Even that day, after the gun battle, Pablo went out back and yelled at his friend, "Damn it, Walker, don't you die. I know you can hear me."

Chapter 4

Corporal Hamms, living the closest, arrived at his home first. Tommy Hamms, thirty-eight years old and on the force for fourteen years, was of medium height, with a bur haircut and clean-shaven face. He had contacted his wife via cell phone and told her to meet him at home. It was 10:55 hours when Hamms turned the corner onto his street. Hamms's house, second on the street, was a very nice three-bedroom Victorian-style home with red brick and a long driveway that reached around to the back yard. The back yard and detached garage were guarded by a decorative wrought iron fence and an electric gate. As Hamms began to pull into the driveway, he noticed that the front door was open just a little. With all his experience, he knew deep down what to expect: the unexpected. He got on the radio and called for additional units to meet him at the corner. Hamms parked his truck just before the driveway, checked his weapon, put in a new magazine, got out, approached the side of the house, and waited for the other deputies.

"To the units responding, no lights or sirens; come in quiet and meet me on the southwest side of the house," ordered Hamms.

THE DRUG TASK FORCE

Two deputies arrived and met Hamms on the side of the house. Watkins, a smaller man with two years on the job, and Sparks, a ten-year vet with the sheriff's office, arrived nice and quiet. Hamms took the lead and the three deputies approached the front door. Hamms, using slow movements around the opening of the door to view the angles into the room, gave directions to Watkins. Watkins went low under Hamms, and Sparks followed Hamms. Inside the living room, all the furniture had been ripped up and thrown about. The computer table was knocked over, and the new fifty-two-inch Sanyo television had a blender in the middle of it. The couch was turned over and the recliner was in three pieces. Hamms motioned to Watkins to come all the way around and cover the hallway. He did. Hamms and Sparks flowed through the living room into the kitchen and dining room. They were quiet and precise and they moved through the clutter of the kitchen and dining room. With all the broken glass and silverware on the floor, it was like a minefield waiting to blow up. Same result; no one else there and a totally demolished room. As the three continued to search the rest of the house, Hamms was concerned as to where their two dogs were. They were not in their kennels in the laundry room, but that question was answered after the men cleared the rest of the house and went to the back yard. The first dog was found floating in the hot tub.

RUSTY POPE

The poor blond poodle mix had been gutted and tied to a brick and dunked in the tub. The hot tub was not turned on, but the usually clean and sparkling water was a dark red with blood. As Hamms was retrieving the lifeless pet, Sparks let out a sigh of disgust when he noticed that the outside grill was on and had a bad odor coming from it. Watkins opened the lid, and there was the other loyal pet, and it too had been butchered and killed. A paper plate was positioned on the side panel, and on this plate was written, "WHERE IS THE WIFEY?" As soon as Hamms read the plate, he was on the phone to his wife. Dawn, a pretty and petite Native American woman with short black hair answered her phone. Hamms instructed her not to come to the house or around to the back yard until he met her. For once there was no debate. Corporal Hamms got on the radio and relayed the information to the rest of the team to be ready for anything. Lowery, Pablo, Humphries, and Roman all acknowledged the radio traffic.

Chapter 5

Joey Brown, also with the sheriff's office for fourteen years, was thirty-five years old and six feet tall with long brown hair and red facial hair. He was the man who knew a little bit about everything and had more useless information than anyone on the team. Brown had arrived at his home just a few minutes after Hamms and before the radio transmission. Brown and his wife arrived home just about the same time, and he held her tightly for a few moments and then met with two deputies that were already at the house. Brown's house, not two years old, was a ranch-style brick house in a very nice gated neighborhood. Brown and his wife Lacey had no kids but were extremely close to his brother's family. Nothing looked disturbed on the outside, and after the three deputies cleared the house, nothing was wrong on the inside. They began packing a few clothes and were ready to load them in their 2009 Chevy Tahoe. The Tahoe was black and tinted out but a real clean family car. The SUV was parked in the driveway, and Brown brought out the first load of clothes. His cell phone began ringing and he answered it immediately. It was Hamms, as he was worried when Brown did not answer his radio. Corporal Hamms relayed the message to Brown as Lacy was bringing out the last load. Lacy, a very pretty super-model-looking, tall woman with long brown hair, asked Joey to unlock the car. Both were standing outside on the porch about twenty-five to thirty feet from the Tahoe. Brown, still on the phone, reached into his pocket and pulled out the car keys, and he then pushed the unlock button on the remote. Lacey was blown back and through the air off the wooden split-rail front deck. Brown also went airborne through the big plate glass window and landed in the middle of the living room floor. Hamms was still talking to Brown when the Tahoe exploded into three pieces and caught fire. The other two deputies in the house heard and felt the blast and ran to the two helpless victims. Brown was cut in several places, including the head, but did not have any life threatening injuries.

Deputy Stricker was the first deputy to arrive at Brown's aid and was trying to calm him down while Brown began yelling for Lacey. Deputy Tippen ran outside and found Lacy on her back in the corner of the front yard fifteen feet from the porch where she was standing just two seconds ago. Tippen reached Lacy, who was not moving but breathing. Tippen gently picked her head up slightly to help her breathe. Lacy, still not conscious, was limp.

THE DRUG TASK FORCE

Brown managed to get to his feet and stumbled outside to check on his wife. Brown yelled at Tippen, and Tippen's return answer was not heard by Brown. Brown saw Tippen answer but did not hear him. Then Brown noticed that he did not hear anything, except a deafening ring in his ears.

As Stricker was helping Brown to his feet, he could hear Corporal Hamms on the cell phone screaming at Brown. Stricker noticed that Brown paid no attention to the phone, so he picked it up and explained to Hamms what had just happened. He explained to Hamms that Brown was bleeding but alive and Lacy had been knocked unconscious with no other serious visible injuries.

Chapter 6

Chance Roman, who lived north of the city, pulled his truck into the driveway of his brown-siding farmhouse. Roman's house was a single-story structure with five acres, a pond, detached garage, and barn. Roman was not a farm boy; he was tall, lean, and a very well-built city slicker. He ran miles every day and pumped a lot of iron in hopes of delaying father time. Roman was strong and fearless unless someone shouted "Snake," then he screamed like a ten-year-old schoolgirl, which meant there were rubber snakes all over the task force office. Roman, being aware of what had just happened to the other team members, reloaded his Glock and made his approach. He was also on edge because around the corner of the street was a Ford Explorer parked on the side road. He had not seen that white 2000 model Explorer in the area before, and it would be a short walk through the woods to his house. As Roman got to the front door, he noticed that the wooden door was open with the storm screen door closed, but he knew that his sixteen-year-old daughter was home, because he called and told her to lock all the doors and windows. As Roman peeked inside, he could see a body of a young man on the floor face down. Roman could see that the boy was not moving, and fresh blood was spilling onto the floor. With dread in his heart and anger on his mind, he quietly opened the front door and reached down to check for a pulse on the young man and could not find one. He lifted the man's head and identified him as Steven, the sixteen-year-old boyfriend of his daughter. Roman heard a door slam, coming from the hallway and one of the bedrooms. A male began to speak with a Spanish accent.

"Come here, little girl, I got your burrito ready," sang the taunting Hispanic male.

Roman did a quick glance and spotted the Mexican male at the end of the hallway. He was tall and heavyset with blue jeans, blue T-shirt, and blue bandana wrapped around his head. The man's back was to Roman, and he was reaching for the closed bedroom door.

"Special sauce with that burrito me *amigo*," Roman whispered.

Roman fired three shots and placed all three in a nice tight pattern in the back of the man's head.

"I asked for special sauce. Oh, there it is," replied Roman.

Roman then began a search of the rest of the house and found his daughter, Julie, in the master bedroom closet. Julie told her dad that Steven had come over to help and stay with her until he got home. Someone knocked on the door, Steven went to look out, the door burst open, and a man shot Steven. She then stated that she ran down the hallway and slammed several doors and then got into the closet and hid under some clothes. Roman hugged his daughter like there was no tomorrow, until Julie began to complain she could not breathe, which was okay with Roman.

Chapter 7

Time was 11:15 hours

Humphries was just putting his truck in park in the driveway of his parents' house. Humphries, recently divorced, was in between houses and women. Freddy Humphries was the youngest member of the team at twenty-four and the shortest. He got measured at least once a week by Pablo, who was glad that Humphries joined so he would not be the shortest. Humphries was also single and ready to mingle, as they say, so that was where he got the nickname Humpme, for he was humping everything in those days. For the short term, he was staying at his parents' house or with one of two girlfriends he was seeing at the time. No one knew where he would be at nighttime, just as long as his ex-wife did not know. That was all that Humphries had to worry about, until the events of that day. Just as he was opening the door, his cell phone rang, and it was his chief from Skiatook.

"This is Chief Spoon; are you okay?" inquired the chief.

"Fine, sir, what's up?" replied Humphries.

"Are you at home yet?"

"Yes, and everything looks fine here," Humphries answered

"Your girlfriend, Rita, was found dead in her apartment. She still had the cell phone in her hand from your last call."

"What, what the hell are you talking about? Rita is dead?"

"I am so sorry; we did not get there in time. Also more bad news. Barbie is also dead. She was gunned down in front of her work, just as she was leaving. So get your parents and get them out of there," the chief stated with remorse.

"Yes, sir, and I will check back with you later," Humphries said as he began to sob. With tears in his eyes for the two women, Humphries got out of his truck and went inside the house. Within a matter of minutes, his parents were loaded up in their car and following Humphries to the sheriff's office.

Chapter 8

Time was 11:20 hours
Pablo had spoken with his wife Karen and agreed to meet at a convenience store a mile from home. When Pablo arrived, Karen was waiting, and they met inside the store and hugged tightly. Pablo gave her an abbreviated explanation and possibly what to expect upon their arrival at home. Karen was a short-haired blonde with good curves and a western spirit as deep as any country girl could be.

Pablo and Karen lived a country life, John Wayne, *Bonanza*, and *The Rifleman*, for Pablo, but on the modern side was Karen, with her Chloe and Coach. They lived in Shell Creek Landing, a city-owned private lake. Pablo was the caretaker for the lake, and the house was a two-bedroom cinderblock home with not much insulation but the view of the lake more than made up for it. They lived a quiet life until the weekends when the grandkids and all the nieces and nephews arrived.

As Pablo was driving and Karen following, they drove to the next-door neighbor's house and parked. Pablo used the garage door opener, and as it rose, the skyline turned black with smoke and red with fire. Neither Pablo nor Karen was injured in the blast. Both just sat in their cars and watched their dream home go up in a loud ball of fire. Pablo smiled, took a drag from his vanilla-flavored Prime Time, a flavored cigar, a swig from his cold Coors light he had just bought at the store, and mumbled to himself, "It's my turn now, mother fuckers, and you ain't ever seen a pissed off Choctaw."

Pablo got out his truck and walked back to Karen's car. She was sobbing, for they had just lost thirty-one years of memories.

"I did not bring this home, so don't even try and blame me," explained Pablo.

"I know, I know, but now what?" replied Karen

"We will get these bastards, I promise," answered Pablo.

Pablo squeezed her hand and kissed her forehead and then returned to his truck and they headed for the sheriff's office.

Chapter 9

Time was 11:15

Mike Lowery and his girlfriend arrived at Mike's house together. Lowery picked her up from work at the county courthouse. Heather, a very pretty and shapely blonde, was doing her internship at the D. A. office in Tulsa. Lowery explained what was going on, and the two found themselves in Lowery's house packing belongings and dog toys.

"You won't need all those law books now; besides I will break ninety percent of the laws in them before the night is over," Lowery smarted off.

"I will leave the books if you leave all that Yankee crap," Heather answered quickly.

"It is not crap, and I have told you that before."

Lowery, a diehard Yankee fan had been at war with Brown, who lived and breathed Texas Rangers baseball, so those two had been going back and forth all summer long.

"Okay, okay, but not my hat, glove, or bat," Lowery pleaded.

In the background, Lowery heard glass packs, a low rumble of a vehicle driving slowly and getting closer. The hair on the back of his neck tingled and his stomach turned as he yelled at Heather, "Get away from the windows." Just as he yelled, gunfire exploded through the house. Lowery hit the floor in the living room and began to crawl to the hallway and then to the master bedroom where Heather was just before the gunfire. He was crawling, plaster and glass was flying all around, and he could hear Heather screaming.

"Heather, Heather, where are you? Answer me," Lowery yelled. After the gunfire has quit and the truck left, he got to his feet and headed toward the bedroom. In the master bedroom, the windows were blown out and the bed was nothing more than foam and springs, but no Heather. Lowery searched on the backside of the bed and then the closet, and there he found Heather, sobbing and cussing under her breath.

"Talk to me. Are you okay?" asked Lowery.

"I think; nothing is hurting or bleeding," Heather said.

She started cussing like a sailor, not at Lowery or the drive-by truck but at everything in general.

"It's okay; I have got you. Relax, it is over for now," Lowery said softly into her ear.

"But it is not over, is it?" implied Heather.

"Not by a long shot, but hurry, they might come back," Lowery said with a voice of reason and determination.

"Look here, what do you think about my books now?" Heather said with a calm voice.

THE DRUG TASK FORCE

At the time the shooting started, Heather was carrying several of her law books, and each book was about four or five inches thick, but now they were riddled with holes. The couple quickly finished loading up and left for the sheriff's office. All six team members had survived the second round of attacks and playing defense against the Mexicans.

Chapter 10

The day had turned from bright and sunny and full of promise to cloudy, dark, and dangerous. The skies were full of rain that had not fallen yet, and there was thunder in the background and a chilling north wind. It was 12:15 hours, and Pablo and his four-car parade was pulling into the gated and now guarded sheriff's office parking lot. Most of the patrol cars were parked along the curb of the street surrounding the entire sheriff's office building. With all the other personal cars in the lot, there was not a lot of parking left close to the doors. In the main lot, the most secured were only about sixty spaces, and this afternoon there were not many left. Pablo had called in a request for four spaces for his group, Pablo, his son and family, and his daughter and her family. Since there were pictures of his grandchildren, Pablo brought everyone, taking no chances. As Pablo was turning off the engine, Lowery and Heather were being chased through the lot by Lady, Lowery's 125-pound Rottweiler, who was hiding in the garage during the drive-by earlier. The office building, including the parking lot, took up half the city block and was three stories tall including the basement. It was uniform brown cinderblock and brick

THE DRUG TASK FORCE

with just a few windows. It was L-shaped and located on the northwest side of downtown Tulsa. Just inside the back gate was the main lot with a couple of loading docks and overhead parking for the upper commanders. There were four doors that led to the maintenance facility and one that led upstairs. There was an elevator opening for the basement and another door for the main entrance into the back of the office where most deputies and the team members entered. Just inside in the back main door was the only elevator, and through a maze of long hallways were the stairs to the second floor. There was a large wood room where the team and family members were gathering. The wood room was named for its decorative wood flooring and the walls, which make the room, look like a 1890s courtroom, with four evenly placed pillars of rough cedar and a floor that had a star-shaped pattern of dark- and light-colored mahogany wood in the middle. The walls were of white knotty pine slabs, to add the authentic western look. The scene inside the wood room looked more like a setting for a social party, with cakes, finger foods, chip dip, pop, and crockpots plugged in everywhere. It was more ready for a party than a place of refuge for the family members. Pablo and his "tribe," as he always described them were greeted by the sheriff himself, Sheriff Charles Larson. He was a very tall, distinguished man in his mid-sixties with gray thinning hair, a Tom Selleck mustache, and big hands. He shook Pablo's hand and introduced himself to the rest of the family.

When they entered the wood room, Pablo and Karen were surprised by all the people and food. Pablo leaned over to Karen and whispered to her. "I thought this was a secret meeting to discuss a safe haven for all the families," Pablo questioned.

"Well, maybe we are staying here until—" Karen lost the words to finish the sentence.

Pablo knew what she meant, "Until it is over."

It was chaos inside the wood room, because Lady liked to eat, and Lowery had his hands full, not with dessert but with a leash and a hunger-crazed dog. A person after only just a few minutes inside could tell this was not a party, but more like a pre-funeral service gathering of family with somber thoughts and soft words being spoken throughout the great wood room until the time for Sheriff Larson to speak. Soon he took the lead and podium and asked for all to grab a chair.

"Ladies and gentlemen, deputies, officers, everyone knows why we are here today. Not only to mourn the death of Randy Hawk, but to pray for our injured and set up a line of defense to protect the families of our fellow deputies. Our deputies in the DTF were ambushed at a suspected drug house, and their lives have come under attack. The ambush was premeditated

THE DRUG TASK FORCE

and carried out with precision. But what these animals did not expect was the amount of professionalism and courage these guys showed in a life-or-death situation. It shows great preparedness in these men to handle a situation, any situation, and to handle themselves when lives are at stake. As most of you know by now, these men's families have been targeted and attacks have taken place. Our duty now is to set up protection for the families of the task force and to allow them the peace of mind so they can do their job and clean our streets of these people. Those of the DTF who want to stay with their families until this is over can and may leave with them as soon as we are ready to move out," Sheriff Larsen said with confidence.

Sue Roman stood up with tears in her eyes and a heavy heart and asked to say a few words. Sheriff Larson gave her the floor.

"I am sorry, sir, for what I am about to say, but those bastards came into my house and were two steps away from killing my—our—daughter, and sir, I want Chance and the rest of these guys to kill them, kill them all, and come back to us after this is finished," Sue demanded.

All the wives and Humphries parents stood up, and all told their respective partners to "finish this," and after several minutes of cheers and ovations, the sheriff took over again. He explained how things would work but did not say where they were taking the families. He then excused the team from the room and told them he would be down to see them when he finished.

The team members all got up and kissed and hugged their family good-bye and promised to see them in the morning. Attending in the wood room were twenty-five uniformed deputies, eighteen members of their SWAT team, nine members of the SOT team from Sand Springs where Pablo was from, six uniformed officers from the Skiatook Police Department, where Humphries was from, and seven police officers from Bixby, where Lowery was from. There were also some FBI agents there, represented by three agents working with the task force but not full time. Matt Chain, Matt Lewis, and Charlie Bright showed up at least once a week or more if the team ran into some exciting cases. It was a good thing to have friends with the fed, because they had all the cool stuff, Pablo said.

Chapter 11

The team headed down to the dugout, a baseball reference to the DTF office. It was named by Brown, Lowery, and Pablo, since those three guys were baseball fans. But Brown and Lowery were nuts for pro baseball; in fact Lowery has purchased World Series tickets just in case the Rangers got to go. The bet was if the Rangers make the series, Lowery had to buy the tickets, and if the Yankees went, Brown would buy them.

Once out of the elevator on the basement level, there was 8,000 square feet of concrete walls and floors. The room was divided into several sections divided by a twelve-foot-high chain link fence, and it was sectioned off for storage of recovered old evidence that was waiting for owners or the auction and also old equipment, paperwork, supplies, and reports. The far end was walled off with concrete blocks and one door clearly marked "DTF Dugout." The lighting in the basement area was poor, with hanging fluorescent lights and a few wall lamps. The air was always cool and damp, and every sound echoed throughout. Once inside the dugout, there were three rooms, the "Bullpen" and the "Batting Cage" were the main two.

RUSTY POPE

The pen had the desks of Sergeant Davis, Corporal Hamms, Lowery, Roman, and Brown, and the FBI guys shared the last desk. The desks were standard fake wood, computer desks with two drawers on each side, three shelves on the top side, and top shelf. In the cage was the desk of Pablo, Humphries, Walker, Hawk, and the assistant, Robert Wayne. Each desk contained the private property of each member and his personal stuff. Of course there were lots of trophy shots of the each man's collectables and the evidence they have collected in the past years. Sergeant's desk was covered with paperwork and the many, many forms the team had to fill out after each search warrant and the C.I.s they employed. Tommy Hamms area had pictures of the Oklahoma Sooners memorabilia, Boomer Sooner this, Boomer Sooner that, which was in direct conflict with Lowery and Pablo, who were both Oklahoma State fans, so there were lots of red and orange colors in both rooms. Lowery had Yankee stuff and O.S.U., and then the usual paperwork.

Brown, on the other hand, had Rangers baseball pictures and wallpapers covering his desk and corkboard wall frames. Roman's desk was just a total disaster, but he was the only one who could find anything in that pile of paper. In the other office, Pablo was orange, and his cork board was covered with photos of him in different hats and clothes. He was

THE DRUG TASK FORCE

very photogenic when it came to modeling bad-guy clothing attire. He had pictures of himself in sombreros, Chinese hats, marijuana pants, and even in a full chemical hazmat suit with gas mask and cigarette stuck in the drinking tube.

Walker had all the latest glass, wooden, and bone smoking pipes, hitters, meth-making glassware, and gadgets.

Humphries had pictures of himself also, but his photos tried to make him look tough and all police business. He was the youngest of the team and was solely there to impress the women, but he was a good officer.

Wayne, on the other hand, was all business, for he had the real job. Wayne's job was hard, as he handled all the phone calls and filing of reports, warrants, and the stats to be turned in to the government for grants. Wayne already had the coffee made for Pablo when the team entered the cage and pen.

The third room was the "Training Room," which was the interview room, and the team members did the decorating themselves. The three walls were painted a light brown and light enough so when they spilled fake blood on the walls, the stains would stick out, and there were several of those stains, and some even on the carpeted floor. A small metal desk sat in the middle of the room, two chairs on one side and one on the other. One side of the room had four very bright lights in the ceiling and two dims lights on the other side. There was a big city phone book, four inches thick, in the middle of the desk. An intercom box and a fairway wood sat in the corner. The fairway wood was the idea of Pablo, who said a good wood can make all the difference in world. One wall had the one-way mirror, so others could watch the interview. There was a fake camera just outside the entry door and one on the inside. As people were being led into the training room, it was explained that the camera was for their protection, but since it was broken, they should tell the truth the first time, because no one would ever know.

There was only one bathroom, known as the "Coaches Box."

As everyone entered, Wayne greeted them all and handed each a packet of information on the two known suspects. Wayne also gave them an update on Walker's condition. He survived the shoulder operation and was going back under the knife within the hour.

Time was 13:00 hours

Each man went to his own desk, fired up his computer, and read through the information packet. Pablo was the only exception to this order; he went to Walker's desk and sat down in his chair. Looking at all the trophies that they had collected for Walker in the previous three years made Pablo feel sick to his stomach. They had become close friends, because they were so much alike. He was sitting staring at the blank computer when Wayne's phone rang.

Wayne answered the phone, and after a brief conversation, he hung up and called everyone together. "Good news for us and bad for them. We have found the truck. It is in the Vacation Inn parking lot on One Hundred Eleventh and East Midland," Wayne informed the team.

"Great! Right in the middle of little Mexico East!" Hamms replied.

"Deputies spotted the truck but did not approach it. They backed off and are sitting out of sight with eyes on the truck," Wayne reported.

"I don't know if I hit anyone when I fired, but we know one is wounded. We know that three were in the truck. Hamms, get a plan. We need to move. Also, Sheriff Larsen wants to speak to us in private before we head out," Sergeant Davis confessed.

"Hey, Sergeant, we don't know where or when they are taking our families," Pablo noted.

"We talked about that and decided it would be better if we, I mean me, too, if we don't know that information, just in case," Sergeant answered.

"Good idea, I guess that is why they pay you the big bucks," Pablo returned.

Burly Matt Chain, skinny Matt Lewis, and Charlie

Bright entered the pen and were bearing gifts, cool stuff, Pablo said.

Roman quickly walked through and told all that he was going to the box.

"Oh crap!" exclaimed Humphries.

"No, number one," Roman stated.

"No! No, I don't mean that," Humphries stated.

Roman left the room in a hurry, like he waited just a little too long, but after only a few seconds, loud angry cussing came from inside the box, but it sounded more like an angry ten-year-old girl cussing.

"I tied a snake to the inside of the toilet lid Friday and forgot all about it," confessed Humphries.

"You better fess up to it, because I am not taking the blame for this one. I will rat you out faster than a trail horse to the barn," Pablo demanded from Humphries.

Roman re-entered and was still cussing, but at Pablo, who was usually guilty of such pranks.

"Tuesday someone is getting their ass kicked," stated a rather angry Roman.

"Humpme did it—not me this time," Pablo stated. He was laughing out loud.

In the "Bullpen" on one of the walls hung a white Magic Marker board where the case agent would draw the layout of the target house, the streets, and the search warrant lineup. Hamms used Google Maps and searched for the Vacation Inn and the layout.

THE DRUG TASK FORCE

"Pablo, you go to the office and find out what room they are in and then keep the office people quiet, and I don't care how. Then we will line up at the door and take them. Be prepared for deadly force, but we need someone alive. It took more than four people to attack our homes. We will line up with Lowery, Brown, Humpme, Roman, me, and skinny Matt. Any of us hurt, immediately transport to St. Michael's hospital. Remember, go slow, identify, and don't miss," stated Hamms with authority in his voice.

"We will wait to drive in until Pablo gets us the room number. Pablo, do your job and do it fast," Roman added.

Wayne entered the room and announced that Sheriff Larsen was there. Sheriff Larsen and Under Sheriff Smith come in carrying gun cases, and they handed out six brand new Glock 40s and four magazines each to all members of the team.

"You guys need more firepower. Also here are six new shoulder holsters," stated the sheriff.

All the guys grabbed the new equipment and began to load and fix their holsters as the sheriff continued to talk.

"I don't need to tell you to be careful, but be safe and smart. The media is beating us up on this."

Brown interrupted. "Are you kidding us? We get shot, blown up, and killed, and this is somehow our fault?"

Sheriff Larsen continued. "The search of the house gave us nothing, not even a seed, crumb, pipe, or even a baggie. We could not tell the media about the duffle bags, so it looks like we are targeting the Hispanics. Even in the jail, the detention officers have been assaulted by Hispanic inmates. Deputies are two per car, as of thirty minutes ago. And one car has been shot at and hit. No injuries, but bullet holes in the trunk of the car. The Hispanic community is turning against us, so we have to stop this in a hurry. The state is still processing the house, and they are at all of your homes doing their parts, but you know policy."

"No, you can't!" Sergeant Roberts said as he jumped out of his chair.

"No, I am not going to do that, but for now all I can do is not answer my phone until oh eight hundred tomorrow. You guys are still out and doing immediate follow-ups. I can hold off the state and the feds for only so long. So by oh eight oh one tomorrow, I will need all your duty weapons on my desk. We have one of the judges on standby, and he knows everything up until now. He will sign search warrants and do phone service warrants. Keep me informed as much as possible. Gentlemen, bend the rules, don't break them. Step on the line, not over it. Keep it legal. With that said, do your job, except do it faster, safer, and get them sons of bitches any way you can. Good luck and good hunting," Larsen said in closing.

THE DRUG TASK FORCE

He went around and shook each of the team member's hands, including a gentleman's embrace and then left the room.

Time was 13:40 hours

In the gun cases were extended barrels for the Glocks that were needed because the FBI guys began to open the gifts and handing out cool stuff. Pablo was like a child at Christmas. Matt Chain, at six feet, two inches, a big man in his mid-forties with short, thinning black hair, handed out radio earpieces that fit in the ear and received and transmitted to and from each piece and to the mobile command van. Skinny Matt, a tall, dark-haired man in his early thirties, gave out directions on how to use the earpieces. Charlie Bright, almost six feet and 200 pounds with ear-length brown hair, asked who was carrying rifles.

"Hamms, Brown, and Roman carry the rifles, while Humphries has a twelve-gauge shotgun and Pablo and Lowery have just the Glocks." Bright handed out three sure-shot suppressors for the rifles, and all got one for their Glocks.

Pablo having tested his radio, began to pack a small gym bag with flex cuffs, bandanas, a large knife, duct tape, screwdrivers, pliers, rubber gloves, a knife, and anything else he could think of.

"What's all that for, or should I ask?" Brown asked.

"I see you are even taking your dull-ass knife," added Roman.

"Going to have to keep those guys quiet, but I will ask first for their cooperation, and the knife is not dull, I tell you," Pablo said as he zipped his bag closed.

Hamms called for everyone's attention and began to give out the assignments. "Remember, Bright and burly Matt in the van with Sergeant; Pablo in the office; Brown, Lowery, skinny Matt, with the ram, Humpme, Roman, the team leader, and me. I will be the ERO, emergency radio operator, inside, and Sergeant has the ERO on the outside. This will be a no-knock warrant and the judge is standing by. Pablo, as soon as you get the room number, call Matt, and Matt will contact Judge Jones for a telephonic warrant. We get the okay, the rest of us will make our approach, and Matt will bust the door. Pablo, you and the command van will protect our backside. Remember, if one of us gets hit, the next two step over and engage while we pull the injured out. This is a no-knock, and be prepared for anything. Go slow, identify, and don't miss," Hamms stated once more in his deep command voice.

Just before the team left, Hamms contacted the marked units that were sitting in the truck and confirmed that the truck was still there. Also reported was that no one has entered or left the room where the truck was parked since they had been there. The guys were reloading their magazines, and the atmosphere in the office turned from idle talk and laughter to dead calm and all business.

THE DRUG TASK FORCE

"Remember, Pablo, we are looking for Edwardo Warez or Ricco Campo," added Hamms.

"Got it, and don't worry. I got ways of making them talk. Remember, I graduated from the Jack Baurer School of interrogation," answered the tough-acting Pablo.

"My bad."

"You got your famous three wood in that bag also?" Roman asked.

"Let's get going; we don't need to give them guys any time to breathe," Hamms reminded all of the team.

Chapter 12

Time was 14:00 hours

The day had turned darker and cooler, and the bottom fell out of the temperature. After a thirty-minute drive, the main part of the parade turned right into a parking lot of a hamburger joint just across the street from the motel. Pablo turned left into the parking lot of the Vacation Inn. It was an L-shaped motel with the parking lot entrance the same as the exit. It had twelve rooms on the bottom of one side and twelve on the other leg, with the same number for the second floor.

Pablo pulled into a space in front of the office and got out of his truck with his gym bag and what looked like a fishing pole carrier. What the bag actually had inside was Pablo's Remington sniper rifle, which Pablo uses as a sniper with the Sand Springs Special Operations Team. Pablo, dressed in khaki pants, a long-sleeved untucked Natural Gas work shirt, and matching ball cap, entered the office and placed his bag on the counter. The rest of the team parked and listening intently as Pablo entered the office. The office area was clean with desert-tan carpet and a Southwest look. Off to the left side of the room there was a sofa, two chairs, a coffee table, and a TV in the lounge area.

THE DRUG TASK FORCE

On the back side of the room was a four-foot counter with a phone, computer, and other motel check-in equipment. On the top counter was a little bell for ringing if no one was present. Pablo relayed the information back to the team that nobody was present. He rang the bell several times and heard someone coming from a back room behind the counter. Pablo was trying to plan for an emergency, just in case the shit hit the fan, when someone started to come through the main door.

"All right, boys, there is a back room that I can't see from out in front of the desk. Hold on. I will let you know how many," Pablo informed the rest of the team.

An older, short Hispanic male came from the back and shut the door to that room.

"I need a room. Got one?"

The Hispanic male just nodded his head yes.

"Two nights, and I need a room close to where my friends are," Pablo said.

The old man just nodded and began to find the room keys and the register, when Pablo added, "My friends are in that brown Ford truck, Warez; I need the room next to them. We work together," Pablo stated.

The old Hispanic man shook his head. "No room, there no room, you must go."

"You just said yes to the room."

RUSTY POPE

Once again the old man said, "You must go, now go."

The back room door opened and two more Hispanic males came out and went to the counter. Those two guys were much taller and younger than the clerk and were dressed the same as the man from Roman's house.

Pablo could see a bulge on the hip of one of the men. With a smooth and quiet voice, Pablo told them, "Easy, boys, just want a room for a couple of nights next to my friends." Just as easy as his voice, Pablo knew he had to make the first move.

Pablo reached under his shirt and pulled his Glock out with the right hand and used his left for balance. He did it so fast he caught the two young guys off guard. Pablo hopped over the counter and kicked the old guy in the chest and knocked him back and down. Then as he was sitting on the counter. He stuck his gun in the face of one Hispanics and shouted at the other, "You move and he dies. *Comprende?* On your knees, fuckers and starts praying. *Habla* English?" Pablo yelled with his not very good Spanish.

Pablo, having made the first move, caught the three Hispanic males off guard and had control of the room. "On your knees, now!" demanded Pablo.

The three men dropped to their knees and placed their hands behind their heads as directed. Pablo then grabbed his bag and hopped off the counter and got

THE DRUG TASK FORCE

behind the three men. Pablo spoke with the team. "I got three of them. Trying to get them cuffed, so give me another minute or two." Pablo made the two young men lie flat and pulled a chrome-plated Smith and Wesson .45 from the waistband of one and then cuffed both men behind their backs. Next he turned to the old man and cuffed him in front, to have access to his hands, if needed. He ordered the two men to roll and sit up with their backs to the wall and pulled out two bandanas and stuffed them into their mouths and used duct tape to secure the gags. It was time for him to focus on the old man and gain the needed information.

"Which room is Warez?"

The old man repeated, "*No hablo*."

"Well, one more '*no hablo*,' and it is going to become uncomfortable and painful. Room number, please?"

"*No hablo, no hablo*," the old man repeated again, and Pablo reached into his bag for the screwdriver. Pablo unscrewed the faceplate off the wall socket that the fax machine was plugged into. He then bared the hot wire and the ground wire and looked at the old man.

"This usually does not hurt the first or even the second time, but by the third and fourth time, the skins starts to burn and the pain increases, so what is the room number?" Pablo said, starting to lose patience.

RUSTY POPE

"*No hablo*" was said again just before the first scream. By the fourth scream, the old man was talking very good English and even told Pablo where the room keys were, not that they were needed. All this was taking place in just a few minutes after Pablo had entered the office.

The team across the street at one point noticed the lights flickering on the vacancy light, and they knew Pablo was working hard.

"Oh no, it looks like Jack Baurer is at work," Lowery stated with a big smile.

Pablo reported back to the team that Warez was in room number thirteen, which was the inside corner room on the ground floor. Pablo was receiving too much information now and had to gag the old man, just to get him to shut up. He told Pablo that there was only supposed to be two men in the room, Campo, who was injured, and a special Hispanic doctor or someone who was taking care of him. As the team moved in, Pablo set up to help watch the entrance to the motel with his 308 Remington sniper rifle equipped with a tripod and twelve-power night vision scope and new suppressor, cool stuff.

The team entered the parking lot of the Vacation Inn in four vehicles. They parked and lined up along the wall opposite the window and next to the door. First Lowery, Brown with the ram, Roman, Hamms,

THE DRUG TASK FORCE

Humphries, and skinny Matt. On the way in, Matt Chain, and Charlie jumped out to help Pablo in the office with his three bad guys, evidence, and watching the back side of the team. Lowery very quietly reached and tried the doorknob, and no luck; the door was locked. With everyone's weapons at the ready, and the day's events still on Brown's mind, he rammed the door, and it broke open with one powerful blow. Lowery first, the team entered, only Roman giving out commands. The room was small and was in the standard shape of any other motel room, one bed, a dresser with a TV on it, two nightstands—one on each side of the bed—and a small refrigerator in one corner. Two chairs sat around a half table in the other corner. A sink, mirror, and countertop led to the bathroom on one side and a closet on the other. The walls were painted a desert tan with two Southwest pictures and dark brown carpet. The bed was a queen size, with one man lying and bleeding in it. The Mexican doctor was sitting in a chair next to the bed tending to the wounds. The doctor was an older gentleman with a green long-sleeved shirt rolled up to the elbows and dark-colored slacks. He was up to his elbows in blood and bandages and guts.

Lowery, Brown, and Roman peeled off to the right as they entered the room, and Hamms, Humphries, and Matt went straight toward the bathroom area.

The doctor, trying to obey Roman's commands, raised one hand and kept his other hand busy inside the wounded man's chest. Lowery's group kept an eye on the doctor and wounded man as the other three approached the bathroom and the closed door. The bathroom door being closed was causing a lot of bad vibes. Hamms slung his rifle on his back and was using his Glock, as was Matt, and Humphries was still using his twelve-gauge pump. Hamms and Humphries were on one side of the door while Matt was on the doorknob side. Matt looked over at the other two men and nodded, signaling time to try the doorknob, and when he tried the door, it was locked. As he was turning the knob, the small room exploded with the sound of automatic gunfire. The door exploded with lead and splinters, all of it directed toward Matt. He was hit with many rounds that were effective even against Matt's bulletproof vest. He fell back and was dead before he hit the floor.

Humphries, with the pump, unloaded his shotgun through the door, and they could hear the groans and thud of a man falling. The door was just a frame as Hamms entered the doorway and fired two more shots to finish off the Mexican assailant.

Roman, as soon as the gunfire stopped, ran over to check on Matt and found the man with as many as six holes clean through his vest and several more

THE DRUG TASK FORCE

elsewhere in his body. The doctor who was used to that kind of violence did not flinch and was still working when Humphries yelled at him to stop and check on Matt. The doctor looked up at Humphries and then looked over at the fallen FBI agent, shook his head, and returned to working on Campo.

Humphries grabbed an open bottle of rubbing alcohol from the bathroom sink and approached the bed. He stood over the wounded Campo's body. "Where is Ware? Where the hell is that bastard? Hey, doctor, get up and go over there and check on Matt, damn it. Check him," Humphries yelled.

Campo looked up and over at Humphries, smiled, and said something in Spanish.

"Wrong answer, you fucker, I too also learned from Jack Baurer."

Humphries' feelings of anger, remorse, and confusion of the day's events tilted the alcohol bottle directly over the wound, ignored the objections of the doctor, and began to pour. The doctor stood up from his chair. Roman grabbed the man by one arm and slung him back onto the carpet. Humphries slowly poured some alcohol into the wound. Campo was a tough, strong forty-year-old Mexican male about six feet tall, but in his physical condition, his pain tolerance was very weak. Roman calmed the doctor down and let him up, and he began to answer some of Humphries' questions.

RUSTY POPE

After about a fourth of the bottle, the team had an address, but trouble was driving up.

Hamms shouted at Campo, the doctor, and even loud enough for people three blocks away could hear. "This is not supposed to happen, and why are these guys carrying AKs? What the hell have we gotten into?"

"The Warez Cartel. They are from the southeast coast area of Mexico. Matamoros was a small city southeast of Laredo, Texas, with a big drug connection in the Mexico State Department. These guys have been in business about a year and are trying to establish a route in Oklahoma and farther north to Chicago. They think they can intimidate and run the police in these small no-name cities along these small state and local highways. They are trying to get an interior base station here in Tulsa. They are holding my brother and his family back in Mexico City, and that is why I am here and not there," confessed the doctor.

"Son of a bitch, no wonder these guys are packing so much firepower," replied Hamms.

"Here are two more AKs, and I don't know how much cash. Drawers are full of twenties and hundred-dollar bills," Brown added.

"Ambulance and ICE agents are on the way," Roman informed the rest of the guys.

"Doc, you need to get out of here and go to the office with us," continued Hamms.

THE DRUG TASK FORCE

"Thank you, but what about Campo?" answered the doctor.

"I don't think that Campo will need your services anymore," Humphries said.

That was all that was said about the previously wounded man in the bed. A very loud explosion came from the parking lot.

"Can you guys hear Pablo cheering in your ear?" Hamms said with a puzzled look on his face.

Through their new earpieces, Pablo, Matt, and Charlie could hear some of what was going on the motel room, and Matt was about to leave the office and help out when an old Ford Ranger arrived at the entrance to the motel. It was an old faded green truck with a driver, passenger, and four other men in the truck bed. They appeared to be on their knees, because only head and shoulders were above the bed wall. They were locking and loading their AK-47s as they stopped just inside the lot and fifty feet in front of the office.

"Hold up, Matt, and take a look at the truck," Charlie said as Matt was going for the door.

"Looks like six bad guys uninvited to our party," Matt said.

"Too many for our Glocks, oh wait, look at that gas cap. I bet one well-placed shot should do the trick," Pablo said with a smile forming on his lips.

Behind his scope Pablo positioned the crosshairs

63

dead center on the cap and squeezed off one silent, well-placed shot, and a split second later, even before the six men knew they were dead, their truck exploded straight up and into a big ball of fire.

"Yep, that should do it," Charlie said with a smile.

"Guess we should get a hold of the fire department," Pablo said as he high-fived Matt.

"Better use a cell phone. The electric around here seems to flicker on and off quite a bit."

"Pablo, status check, and what the hell is all the cheering and the explosions about?" quizzed Hamms.

Pablo heard the request through his earpiece and was excited to relay the good news.

"We are okay, three suspects detained. We have recovered a very large amount of money and a couple of handguns. Also Matt and Charlie have found four ledgers with names and different addresses in town. Looks like a stash house for drugs and money. How are you guys, with all the gunfire?"

"Two dead suspects, one reliable witness, several guns, and also a large amount of cash. One of the dead guys is Campo."

"Did you hear that truck blow up?"

"What truck? What was that all about?"

"Well, after you guys finished shooting everyone, this truckload of mad Mexicans pulled into the lot. Six of them in all, and they were loading their AKs, and I shot the gas tank out from under them. They went up like a Roman candle."

"Sometimes I worry about you, Pablo. I need you guys to listen up; Matt was killed in our raid. He was killed trying to open a locked door. I will explain later, just hurry up and gather what you need and get back to the office. Sergeant will take care of the clean-up," ordered Hamms

"Roger. Did I hear you right?"

"Yes, now hurry."

Pablo walked by the three suspects, who were sitting in the lounge area in the floor duct taped together with their backs to each other. Pablo reached out and kicked one of them, not hard, but hard enough to make them grunt and groan with pain. Matt and Charlie were in the back room when Hamms gave them the report about skinny Matt, and Pablo could hear a screams of pain, anger, and slamming of furniture.

"Sergeant, are you still in the van and close?" asked Hamms.

"Roger, and I copy your last," answered Sergeant

"Can you start fire, ambulance, and ICE to take care of Pablo's detainees? We will transport the doc with us."

"They are already on the way."

"Thank you."

The mood for the team again turned from good

to bad in a single moment as the doorknob tuned, so did the fate or luck of the DTF. As the men loaded up and left the Vacation Inn, each of them was thinking about their friend Matt Lewis, Brown, and Lowery had a good relationship with Matt, as they were all close in age and had similar likes. They were always planning the parties that the team had, and their wives took pictures, which led to some very embarrassing moments the day after. It was a long, quiet drive back to the office in every vehicle.

Chapter 13

Time was 15:20 hours

A light rain began, darker clouds took over the skies, and the temperature kept falling as the team was on the way back to the dugout received some good news. Walker had survived the second and last surgery and was in the recovery room. Pablo smiled with the news then lit a cigarette and dedicated the first drag to his friend Johnny Walker.

The team arrived back at the office. All were carrying evidence from guns, cash, and notebooks, and the doctor was being guarded closely. The parking lot was nearly empty, for most of the deputies were on patrol or set up for protection of the families who had been moved half an hour earlier. The bad guys' bodies had all been transferred to one hospital, while the law enforcement bodies and injured were sent to another hospital, to protect their families from a possible ambush.

Time was 15:40 hours

The door to the dugout closed behind Humphries, who carried in the last bundle of evidence. Wayne greeted the team in a somber low voice, because he too had heard the news about Matt, the FBI agent.

"Corporal Hamms, it is getting worse out on the streets. The media has turned on the Hispanic community and are reporting the facts and not fiction. They are talking about an ambush, and the bad guys did fire the first shots. The jail is on lockdown, and they are starting to gain back some control," reported Wayne.

"I did not know they had lost control."

"Yes, almost a full-blown riot in the jail."

"Shit, is the whole city going crazy, or what?"

"Two more patrol cars came under fire. Mexicans are targeting only county units, not even bothering the T P D cars or officers."

Brown jumped in. "Well, they declared war on the wrong agency. I can tell you that right now."

"Let's get this evidence organized, and let's not worry about counting the cash. Wayne, can you look over these books? They are written in English and Spanish," Hamms stated as he took charge of the office.

"Right away," answered Wayne

Wayne, a tall, silver-haired man of sixty-eight years, was a retired border patrol officer from El Paso. His wife was from Tulsa, which was why he landed there after retiring with twenty-six years in law enforcement.

"Wayne, can you take them back to the training room with the doc and see what you can find out, and real fast?"

THE DRUG TASK FORCE

"The doc?"

"Yes, he is on our side now."

"Right away, oh yes, the Mexicans out east are starting fires and creating quite a disturbance."

"I can't help that right now. Do your best, and fast."

Out east at 15:00 hours ,another county patrol came under attack. The patrol car was shot at, the tires were shot full of holes, the driver was hit and wounded, and the second deputy was killed. The Mexicans took the wounded deputy out of the disabled patrol car and hanged the deputy by the neck right there from the traffic light pole. Citizens watched in horror and placed several 911 calls, but the responding units were too late. The deputy was just in his third year on the force, and he and his wife had twin daughters. A McDonald's and Arby's were robbed and the stores were set on fire. These stories came from the local news station on TV and radio talk shows. The massacre was done by low-life Mexican scum bags, not by the people the DTF was tracking.

The Drug Task Force was a multi-jurisdictional task force made of up different agencies. Sand Springs, where Pablo was from, was a city of 19,000 people west of Tulsa. Pablo was a twenty-year veteran with the department and had been married for more than thirty years to the same woman. He was the only one still on his first marriage in the task force. He was fifty years old, and most said they were still waiting for his mature age to catch up with his real age.

Humphries, in his third year, was from Skiatook, a smaller lake town north of Tulsa. This town had grown by leaps and bounds the last few years, in large part due to the lake's gaining popularity. The lake, simply known as Skiatook Lake, was a large fishing lake stocked with bass. Humphries was not native to Skiatook but fit right in with the community. He was on his second marriage, but to the same woman, different category, according to Pablo. At the present time and for the last nine months, Humphries was single and ready to mingle, hence the nickname "Humpme."

Mike Lowery was from Bixby, a community out south of town, and he had eight years on the job. All eight were with Bixby, and he was single also, but had a steady girlfriend. In fact they were a couple just looking for a date to get hitched. Lowery said he was not going to tell anyone and just get married, because he did not want the rest of the guys to kidnap him the night before. That issue had been brought up more than once in conversation.

Then there were the guys from the county, with Hamms a corporal with fifteen years of experience and five on the task force. Roman, who was the leader in marriages, with four, and four children that he knows of, had over twenty-four years with the sheriff's office.

THE DRUG TASK FORCE

He was a big man who liked to lift weights and run. Joey Brown, thirty-five years old, knew more worthless information than anybody in the world. He was on his second marriage and once gave advice to Lowery. "Marry the second time for money, and the love will soon grow."

Those guys had several things in common, but one of the main reasons they were so successful was that they all had a sense of humor, which in their line of work can hold a team together through many bad times. They never wore their feelings on their sleeves, for if they had, it would show a weakness, and the rest of them would have circled like hungry shark after bait fish. Counting the FBI guys, the ATF, and the three reserve deputies assigned to them, there were fourteen people that made up the DTF.

Hamms began to talk with Brown. "Broad daylight, and this shit happens. This is just what the cartel wants, total chaos and fear throughout the city."

"I am looking up the address we got from Campo, on Google Earth."

Pablo just entered into the room after separating the evidence. "What address are you talking about, Joey?"

"We got a few answers from Campo before he died of alcohol poisoning."

"Alcohol poisoning? Oh no, I got to hear this!" Pablo said, shaking his head.

"I will explain tomorrow," Humphries stated from the other room.

Roman from his desk in the corner asked, "Pablo, how come the lights were flickering in the motel office?"

Pablo quickly fired back, "We were working on one of the wall sockets, and the man kept touching the bare wires. I warned him, but he could not understand English, at first."

Doc and Wayne were going over the books, and Doc was explaining what he already knew about the cartel to Wayne.

"Already thirty to forty men in Tulsa and more close by?" asked Wayne.

"Yes, and they are well financed and equipped. I do not think they have anyone on the payroll as yet, but that is what some of the cash is for. They were saying something like the American police are more expensive than the Mexican police."

"Good, glad to hear that they don't have those kinds of connections, yet."

"But with this kind of cash, it is only a matter of time before someone gets greedy."

"Yes, and time is running out," agreed Wayne.

Wayne left Doc alone for a minute and re-entered the bullpen with the rest of the team to report about two addresses that seemed to be very important. One

THE DRUG TASK FORCE

address was a grocery store and the other was a small one-story house. Both addresses were out east and around where all the trouble was taking place.

"Good news, we now have three places to go and find the other thirty or forty bad guys and Warez himself," reported Hamms.

"Wait, you know how many men we are up against?" Pablo said with a look of confusion.

"Yes, and we are up against a Mexican drug cartel called the Warez Cartel."

"The hell you say!" said Pablo, really confused now.

"Yes, and that is where we are sending their bodies, straight to hell."

"Preach on, brother!" Lowery said from his desk.

"Okay, here is the address, two two one nine East Seventy-ninth Court, a single-story home with a two-car garage," Brown said as he finally found the maps on the computer.

"Damn it, it is at the end of a cul-de-sac. A great place for the bad guys to set up another ambush and get us in a crossfire from both sides of the street," Roman said as he looked at the map.

"We now know what and who we are fighting. They have lots of firepower, but remember we are attacking, so we still have some element of surprise," Hamms said as he was trying to calm the guys down. Hamms was looking around the room at the guys who had gathered by Brown's computer to look at the map. Hamms could see all the emotions going through the guys from disbelief, anger, and some confusion on how and why the cartel had brought this war on them, just a group of men trying to do a job of protecting the citizens and stopping the flow of illegal drugs into their city. With that thought, he asked and answered his own question. Hamms, sat with head in hands, thinking how could this group of men defeat a cartel, when Brown broke the silence and began to speak. "There are eleven homes on the street, and our house is in the middle of the cul-de-sac. The other ten homes are across from each other, so it is a natural funnel."

"How about putting Pablo and Stevens, our sniper, in the back of a truck? Each of them can cover their own side of the street, and they both have a spotter and fully automatic M-sixteen for backup," Roman said, thinking out loud.

"Good. They can be at the back of the line," Hamms confirmed.

"Once we turn the corner, we are in the open and vulnerable."

"Okay, once we turn the corner, we are compromised and need to haul ass to the house and get inside," Roman added.

"We will drive slower and protect the street and secure our way out," Pablo returned.

THE DRUG TASK FORCE

"Once we are inside the house, shoot and don't miss, but we need this guy," Brown continued.

Brown was handing out pictures he had copied from the computer and NCIC records, photos of Warez and a guy name Felipe Ramirez. Felipe was reported to be a general for the cartel and the executioner general.

"Pablo, as soon as the other guys get here, get them briefed and ready to go. We need to get busy," Hamms commanded.

"Right, the more time we sit here, the more time they have to get ready for us," Pablo answered back.

Sergeant Davis just arrived back at the dugout and gave them an update on what had taken place in the aftermath at the motel. Hamms in turn gave the sergeant the plan for the team's next move and gave him the information from the doctor and Wayne and what they have discovered.

"Guys, listen up! We are now against a group of people who do not understand law and order. We may need to pull out and let the feds and the military handle this from here on out. Your opinions?" Sergeant Davis asked.

Lowery immediately stood up and sounded off. "Sergeant, they have killed our team member, shot and blew up our families and homes, scared our town, and are trying to kill us. I say that they have brought this on themselves, and they need to know that we are not going away, and I for one am going to finish this."

Roman continued, "No way. We are in the middle of this, and we are going to finish it our way."

"Sir, we are living in America, not Mexico, and we are a civilized nation and people. We will rise up and not be denied the freedom and security that we had yesterday. I am vested in finishing this fight," Humphries added.

"That is a good point, Sergeant, but this is our city, not theirs," Hamms replied.

Pablo, being Pablo, shook his head, stood up, raised his arms palms up, and said with a deep, meaningful voice, "No need to say anything more. Let's finish this."

"Those bastards owe me a new house," Brown joined in.

Matt and Charlie returned to the dugout. After they had left the motel, they went to the hospital with their partner, Matt Lewis. They both were still grieving the loss of Matt, but had a fire in the pits of their stomachs, a fire that was burning, and only revenge and justice would quell that fire. They were caught up on the information that had been gathered and the ensuing raid planned for the flop house.

The other deputies arrived, and Pablo called them to his office area. "Stevens and I are the snipers. Smith, you are my spotter. Riley, you will be with Stevens, and Bowls, you are the driver. We will be in the back of a truck and will be last in the parade. Look at the board and get your plan ready. We need to leave as soon as you guys are ready," Pablo said as the others were gearing up.

"I will take the left side of the street," Stevens said.

"I will have the right side, and we will have M-sixteens at the ready, if needed. Rick here is our play."

To Rick, Pablo gave very specific directions. "I shoot left handed, so be on my right shoulder. As we turn the corner, each house is one, three, five, seven, nine. You good with that?"

Rick Smith nodded in agreement, and Pablo continued, "Each window of each house starts right to left, one, two, three, and so on, so house one window one, you tell me one- one, and I will shoot the fucker who shows up at that window. These are pictures of our houses, so when we drive through, you say in my right ear where you want me to shoot. Anyone who shows his head gets a hole in it, Does not matter who or why they look, just wrong place, wrong time."

"Good plan, just hope that it is a smooth ride," Smith answered.

"I got four magazines with five rounds. If we need more firepower, grab the sixteen and cut loose. I have six twenty-round magazines."

Stevens and his spotter, Riley, were finishing their

briefing, and the five of them began to gather up their equipment.

Time was 16:40.

Hamms gathered everyone in the bullpen and prepared them with what they were up against and then gave out the assignments.

"All right, two per car, with Brown and Lowery first. Brown has the ram. Then Roman, team leader, and Humphries, with the shotgun, will be second. Matt, Charlie, and I will be next, followed by Pablo in the sniper truck. No matter what Pablo and his truck encounter, we have to secure the house. We could use it for our Alamo, if needed, but we need the house. Pablo, you guys are on your own out there until we get to the house. We are going to haul ass after we make the corner. Any questions?"

"Shock and awe, baby, shock and awe," Pablo said with excitement.

"We leave here in five minutes," Hamms finished.

The phone rang, and sergeant answered and told everyone that Walker was trying to wake up. Then he called the judge for the warrant.

Chapter 14

While all the planning and strategizing was going on, Wayne went back into the training room with Doc, as he was eager to learn much more about the invading Warez Cartel. The doctor, a tall, lean Hispanic man in his late fifties with graying hair and mustache, was born in Texas and raised in Mexico. He had gone to college and medical school in the States. The doctor did have a nice life in Mexico, married and four children, and living and practicing his trade in Matamoros, Mexico, which was just across the border of the southwest Texas towns of Mercedes and Kingsville. Until six months ago, when the cartel needed his services along the new northern trade route, they raided the doctor's town and killed his wife and kids, but with nothing to live for, Doc told them no. The doctor changed his mind when he received pictures of his brother and his brother's family being held hostage. He believed that his brother and family were dead, but kept doing his job for the cartel just in case. Wayne had learned that this new Warez Cartel split from the Gulf Coast Cartel a little over a year ago. Edwardo Warez became too big for the GCC, and when the GCC wanted him gone, Warez split and went underground before he could be taken out. He took Ricco Campo and his two brothers, Philippe and Julio, and his lifelong friend, Jamie Esponza. Ricco and Jamie became the generals, and they started recruiting or kidnapping older teenage boys for their cartel. They gave the recruits whiskey, weed, and women. What teenage boy would refuse those perks? Then they introduced them to guns and to kill or be killed, and now the boys knew only three things: smoke, fuck, and kill. They first started with just a simple road trip to Chicago, winding their way through Texas, Oklahoma, Missouri, and Illinois. They took over $100,000 up there and set up with a buyer and came back the same way, only faster, and it took two nights. They would only travel at night and in the early morning rush hour traffic and would sleep and rest during the day in two-bit rat trap no-tell motels. Then they started bringing up the boys and taking over these small motels and gas stations, Mom and Pop operations only. Warez and Ricco would buy the police department items that they needed, like cars, lights, and sirens for those cars and police supplies such as vests and individual items. They were Santa Claus to those little communities, and then the police started looking the other way when shipments came through town. They would think if they don't stop the trucks, then they would not know that they were breaking the law.

THE DRUG TASK FORCE

Up until now they were having no trouble establishing their line, but when they got to Tulsa, they were having trouble getting a foothold in town. There was a big gap in their line from there to Neosho, Missouri, and then clear all the way to Illinois. Wayne was wondering why there was a gap in this area, and Doc explained that the feds and local police departments worked too close together, like the way the FBI and the drug task force worked together and shared information. Too many eyes were watching the police up there, they said, so they were there trying to map out another route. "We were to leave this month, and then you guys showed up and were getting too close. Warez and Ricco had already showed cash and bought your guys' information and took pictures and set up your families for a big show of force. When Warez found out who the informant was, he put this plan into action and tried to scare or kill you guys away from him and his route. But your guys were too good this morning at the house and then at the motel. Missed Warez by five minutes at the motel, and now you guys have them worried and mad because no one has stood up against them and fought back."

Wayne, taking all this information in, said, "Well, they certainly shot at the wrong group of guys. I have never seen them act this way. I mean they are out for blood."

"That is good, because Warez has lost two of his generals and is scrambling for cover, and if he gets to worried he will go back underground and be even more dangerous," Doc answered.

"These guys are getting ready for war and leaving now as we speak."

"Good, they need to stay after him, and he will make a mistake."

"He already did," Wayne stated as cold and hard as he had ever spoken before.

During this time Doc had to make a couple of trips to the bathroom, and after the first time, Wayne just let the doctor go by himself. The trips were not long, but Wayne did notice something strange about Doc's behavior each time he came back.

As soon as the team had arrived back at the dugout and Hamms confirmed that the address was a good target, he sent an unmarked unit to sit at the house and report any movement. As the team was making its final equipment check, Hamms received a phone call from the unmarked unit. "Ten-four, we will leave in the next five minutes and fifteen to get there, so let me know. All right, boys, we have four young Hispanic males that just arrived in two cars and are parked in the driveway of our target house," Hamms informed the team.

THE DRUG TASK FORCE

"Saddle up, boys, for *Shock and Awe II*," Pablo added to what Hamms was saying.

In four trucks and Sergeant Davis in the command van, the team members left the dugout in search of Edwardo Warez and anyone else who happened to get in their way.

Chapter 15

Time was 16:55

The parade was pulling into a shopping mall parking lot just three blocks from the target house. Pablo and his group were setting up in the bed of the truck and making ready. Hamms got his third call, and the Mexicans were loading up the cars and getting ready to leave.

"Let's do this," Brown said as everyone headed for the parking lot.

As the parade left the lot, the sky began to turn darker and darker by the minute, and now the time was around 17:10 hours. The daylight began fading with each passing tick of the clock.

In the back of the truck, Pablo leaned over to Stevens and said, "Hey, Stevens, I hope there is a little light left for our spotters."

"Yeah, could be trouble if they can't see," Stevens answered as he too was wondering the same thing.

The line of cars was about to turn left onto E. 79th Court, and the target house was a quarter of a mile straight away. The street was quiet and no cars parked on the curbs, no obstructions, but not any cover either. There were a few trees in the front yards of the

THE DRUG TASK FORCE

houses, and two of the homes had no lights on and no cars and un-mowed lawns, giving the appearance of vacant homes. On Pablo's side of the street there were three brick homes and two brown-siding homes and all brick houses on the other side of the street for Stevens. All of the homes in the cul-de-sac were single-story homes with gray shingles and at least two of the homes on Stevens's side had front yard chain link fences and children's toys scattered about. All the homes were small 1,200- to 1,600-square-foot homes with three bedrooms and one or two bathrooms. Two of the homes had garages that had been changed into dens, with no garage doors.

The breeze turned into a steady wind and the temperature had dropped as suddenly as the mist had turned into a sprinkle, just enough to make a driver turn intermittent wipers to medium.

The team made the left turn and sped down the cul-de-sac to the target house without being fired on. Pablo's truck putted slowly down the middle of the street at about seven to ten miles per hour. Pablo's spotter said "One, two," and Pablo got on target but did not fire.

A small boy looked out the front storm door at the weather and the speeding car. A loud thunder roared to the north and lightning flashed across the horizon, and for an instant Pablo thought he had pulled the trigger.

Stevens's spotter said, "Two-two," and a split second later, the rifle roared to life and Stevens mumbled to himself, "One down." The truck approached the end of the street and Stevens again fired, two down. No one showed up on Pablo's side of the street to be shot when the truck had reached the target house. The truck parked in front and parallel to the house, and the four men bailed out and took up positions of cover behind the truck to provide cover and additional manpower to the entry team if needed.

"Stevens, I think they all got on your side of the street thinking you might miss and I would not," Pablo said to Steven as they took their positions.

"Funny guy, Pablo," Stevens fired back.

"I was sure nervous driving slow through an ambush," Bowls pitched in.

Both Stevens and Pablo answered, "We had your back."

From looking at Google Maps of the house, the team could tell that there were two front windows, so they decided to add their own chaos to this entry. Brown and Lowery in the first truck jumped the curb and stopped ten feet away and directly in front of the house. Just as they were stopping, one bad guy carrying a duffle bag came to the front door. He dropped the bag and yelled out to the others in the house and ran back in.

THE DRUG TASK FORCE

"Wrong choice, bitch!" Lowery yelled at the Hispanic male as he ran inside the house. Brown ran to the front door and Lowery to the right side window. Humphries and Roman in the second truck stopped in the yard also, to the left of Brown's truck. Humphries went to the left window and Roman to the door. Hamms parked his truck in the middle of the driveway, blocking both bad guys from leaving, if they made it that far. Hamms, Matt, and Charlie all ran to the front door. They heard the first shot of Stevens and then the thunder and a second shot, just as Hamms, Lowery, and Humphries threw their flash bangs into the house.

Flash bangs are military-style grenades that create a very bright flash of light and a deafening bang. The bright light is like a flash bulb going off in front of your eyes. You can't see anything but white dots for minutes. The bang is so loud that if not ready, it can take away your hearing for up to an hour, and you hear nothing but loud ringing in your ears.

The bangs were the idea of Roman, who loves to throw the bangs. Three loud explosions in a 1,500-square-foot home will make anyone go deaf and blind and take cover.

The team members entered the house as Pablo's truck pulled to the curb and parked. With Lowery first, Brown, Roman, Humphries, Hamms, Matt, and Charlie next, the team entered the living room, and off to the right was the dining room and kitchen, which usually led to a garage door. Lowery and Brown went to the kitchen and dining room area, while Roman and Humphries cleared the living room. Not much furniture, much like the first house, only plastic chairs and a table, but a first-class, big bucks, big screen TV mounted on the wall with a PSP, Play Station hooked up. With only a ceiling fan light on and not much light from the windows, the room was dark as Brown and Lowery made their way to the kitchen. Hamms, Matt, and Charlie had held at the front door until the living room was cleared, and then they moved up with Roman and Humphries, who were holding the hallway until the kitchen and dining room were secured. Brown and Lowery had made it through the kitchen and were heading to the garage. They opened the door and made entry into a completely dark garage, and the garage was not for cars, but a junk storage room. There were boxes and plastic containers all stacked up in rows, with only a single-file aisle in between the rows. Brown reached out and hit the light switch, and one target appeared in the far left corner by the garage door. Brown saw him first and yelled then fired two bursts, and the target, a young Hispanic male fired back. The bad guy's shots were from another AK-47, and he fired until he fell back into several boxes. Brown and Lowery took cover and returned more fire, not hitting anything except Sheetrock. It was silent for a few seconds until the silence was broken by the sound of a person taking his last breath in this life.

Brown and Lowery moved up to discover a Hispanic male about twenty-something lying on his back still clutching his AK. Brown from just inside the garage shouted to the rest of the team that the garage was cleared and that he and Lowery were okay.

Humphries pointed to an open bedroom door and then the second open door, so he and Roman entered the bedroom first. There was only a mattress on the floor and no one hiding in the empty closet. Hamms, Matt, and Charlie moved up to cover the hallway as the other two men entered the room. Roman shouted "Clear," and the team moved up to the second room. Hamms and Matt entered the second bedroom, which had one mattress, a dresser, and a closed closet door. As Matt was reaching for the door, they heard someone in the closet and a sound, the same sound that Matt heard just before, the sound of someone charging a rifle.

"Come out, we know you are in there," Hamms shouted.

Another sound, and this time the sound was loud and distinctive.

"He is charging his weapon," Matt yelled out to Hamms.

Both men opened fire into the closet door and

through the thin Sheetrock walls. Both men emptied their Glocks and took cover and listened, but nothing, not a sound, except their own breathing. Matt opened what was left of the closet door, and they found a twenty-something Hispanic male clutching his AK, except his AK had a round jammed in the ejection port.

"Poor bastard, you should have practiced more with your gun," Hamms said to the dead man.

As soon as Hamms was finishing his sentence, Roman and Humphries began yelling, "Hands up, let me see your hands," and two more Hispanic males, both in their twenties, come out of the third bedroom.

"Smart move, you chicken bitches, now get out here." Roman ordered the men out of the room.

Hamms, Matt, and Charlie finished clearing the house, and Roman and Humphries moved the two prisoners into the living room and handcuffed them.

"Get their cars keys or find them, and we will load these men in the van and drive their cars to the office. They already collected most of the evidence for us," Hamms told Brown and Lowery.

Roman slapped one of the men on the back of the head and said, "*Gracias.*"

"Coming out, and found the keys," Charlie said as he came out of the house. The team loaded up, with Lowery and Humphries driving the two Mexican-owned cars.

THE DRUG TASK FORCE

"Now this is more fucking like it, two captured bad guys and two dead, and we get to go home and eat dinner," Hamms said with a loud and victorious voice.

They sped out of the cul-de-sac as fast as they had come in.

The time was 17:40 and the rain and wind had quit.

Chapter 16

It was 18:10 as the team arrived back at the sheriff's office. Sergeant Davis had the two prisoners in the van and unloaded them and took them to a separate side of the office and held them for the ICE agents. The team entered the dugout and was greeted by Wayne and Doc and hot pizza, cold pop, and hot coffee for Pablo.

"Corporal Hamms, Doc and I put together a flow chart with pictures of the Warez Cartel on the board," Wayne informed Hamms as they went into the office.

"Great, that will save us some time and give us some idea of who we are up against."

"I have learned a ton about this organization from Doc and the ledgers."

"Anymore locations we need to take out? And please, no bad news."

"There is a convenience store that needs to be hit, probably next. Doc says it is a warehouse for drugs, guns, and other weapons. Also says Ed might be there re-supplying his men," Wayne stated with a sense of accomplishment.

Wayne and Doc led Hamms into the bullpen and explained the board as the rest of the team went in.

THE DRUG TASK FORCE

They were grunting under the strain of the weight of the duffle bags. They dumped the bags in the middle of the room with a sigh of relief. They begin to open the five bags and were overjoyed at what they were finding.

"I think we ought to get to keep what is in our own bag," Brown said boastfully.

"Just my luck all I got is weed," Roman whined.

"Wish me luck, oh shit only kilos of ice," Pablo grumbled.

"I got cash, and lots of it, Merry Christmas to me, suckers." Brown whooped and started to dance.

Humphries danced as well, because his bag had cash also.

"More stinking weed, just my luck, and I just quit smoking weed yesterday," Lowery said with a frown on his face and a joke in his heart.

All the guys were acting out and slamming each other as a release of the pressure that was getting to all of them. Only Roman had shot and killed another human being, so this was new to all of them.

Hamms then made an announcement, and all returned to their new reality. "Turn the radio up and listen TPD and county units in pursuit of a carload of Hispanics. Don't know if they are related to ours."

The radio blared as the officers were giving directions of travel and other information about the chase.

RUSTY POPE

"Guys, you need to look at this board in here," Hamms said.

Matt and Charlie entered and froze in their tracks as they saw money, drugs, and cash all over the floor.

"Looks like my bachelor party a few years ago," Matt joked.

"First, second, or third time?" Charlie replied with laughter.

"Always the smart ass, aren't you?" Matt fired back.

"Join us in here," someone shouted to the two FBI agents. "You got to see this."

They entered the bullpen and saw the elaborate diagram on the board. They stopped and stared alongside the other guys. Doc explained the board to all the guys about what role each of the generals and captains played in the cartel. "The third general, or the last one still alive, is also the executioner. His role is to execute all prisoners after he's tortured them for information. Felipe Ramerez is the bloodiest of them all. The three captains keep an eye on the day-to-day business operations regarding weed, ice, and the money. Each captain is also a recruiter for his unit." Doc also explained about the tattoos the gang wore.

"I was wondering about that. They all have, tattoos that say 'seventy-seven,' but in different colors," Roman said.

THE DRUG TASK FORCE

"That is their highway to the U.S., and the colors are who they work for, green for weed and red for blood and so on," Doc answered and continued. Doc then talked about the addresses on the board and what roles they played. The convenience store was a logical place to hit next, being a supply store. The other address the team was looking at was not an office building but a warehouse that belonged to the generals. The team decided to hit the store then regroup quickly and hit the house, if they still had not caught up with Warez.

"There is one other thing that bothers me; Hamms. Why so much red and all of this Sooner stuff?" Doc asked seriously.

"Well, if I have to explain it to you, you are not smart enough to understand it."

"I watch football some, and the Sooners are nothing to be so proud of," Doc said, still not knowing who he was talking to.

The guys in the room, hearing that statement, groaned with disbelief at what they had just heard. Hamms was still trying to be nice, but all he could come up with was, "Boomer Sooner bitch! You are a guest in my house and don't forget it."

The guys bowed their heads, and some snickers came from the back. Hamms pointed at the door, and after one awkward second, Doc left the room.

"Wow! That was as tough as I have ever seen you act out against someone against OU," Brown said to Hamms.

"Shit, he is a Longhorn, and actually I was trying to be nice."

Chapter 17

Time was 18:30 hours

"Twenty minutes, and we are on the road again," announced Hamms.

Hamms gave the lineup with Lowery, Pablo, Brown, Roman, Humphries, then himself, with Matt and Charlie taking the back and the sergeant in the command van. The store was on the corner of 111th and Roosevelt, a 4,000-square-foot building with three concrete walls and a glass front wall.

"We are going to need window breakers and flash bangs again. They worked real well the last time," Humphries said as they began with their plans.

"Yes, and this time me and Roman with the umps, and we will provide cover fire if needed," Hamms added.

"Hump Me and the shotgun for close encounters. Brown, Pablo, and Lowery will stay with your Glocks." Roman confirmed.

"Three trucks only, Pablo, Brown, and Lowery in one and Roman and Hump Me in one, and I will take the FBI with me," instructed Hamms.

"Boys, pursuit ended with crash, gunfire, and four dead bad guys. No good guys injured," Wayne interrupted. "But none of the bad guys had tattoos."

RUSTY POPE

Cheers all around the room.

"Just plain ol' bad guys out for a joyride, I guess," Pablo said as he grinned and winked at Wayne.

Pablo. staring at the address and the store, smiled and called Hamms back into the room. "Hamms, I got an idea of how to surprise attack these bastards."

"I can't wait to hear this."

"About a block away, Brown and Lowery pull the back seat down and crawl into the bed of my truck. I will back into the glass front wall, and when I stop, they will lift the lid, throw the bangs, and close the lid. After the bangs go off, they will open up, and one right, one center, and me on the left. The others will cover the corners, and we will work our way to the back of the store. *Shock and Awe Three*, babies."

"We should have played your tune 'Another One Bites the Dust,'" Lowery said in jest.

Hamms agreed and gave Sergeant the lineup and details of the new raid plan and the team suited up again.

With the manner in which the team was getting information and rapid response to that information, the cold pop and hot pizza sure made a difference in their energy levels. Before the break they were dragging and lost in their feelings for the loss of their friends, but now they reached a new high, and the team was gearing up with the hope that a nightmare was nearing an end.

Chapter 18

Time was 18:50 hours

Once again after the team made a decision on where to go next, Corporal Hamms sent an unmarked vehicle to get eyes on the target location. The sergeant had made the phone call to Judge Jones and gotten the telephonic warrant, so the team had the warrant in hand. Since the time change had just occurred the past weekend, the sky was already dark from the low ceiling of clouds, and the north wind was blowing cold air. The team loaded up and pulled out of the parking lot as another very loud thunder clap exploded, almost as if to signal another attack. The rain had quit, but the roads were still wet and slippery. While en route, the team witnessed one crash as it happened, and Hamms radioed it in to dispatch. After ten more minutes of driving, the team parked two blocks away, and inside Pablo's truck, Brown and Lowery pulled down the back seat, turned on a flashlight, and crawled into the bed of the truck. On the radio, the unmarked gave an update that a tricked-out blue Dodge king cab truck with two Hispanic males just left, and someone inside had just turned off the lights. Pablo leaned toward the back seat area and said to Lowery and Brown, "You guys ready yet?"

"If you are waiting for us, you are backing up. Hit it!" Lowery answered.

Pablo pulled just past the entrance and stopped. Roman lefts enough room for Pablo to back up into the entrance.

"Hamms, are you guys ready?" Pablo said on the radio.

"Lead the way," Hamms answered back.

The store was approximately 150 feet from the curb and had two lights on the inside of the store. No cars were in the lot, only two rows of four gas pumps, and there were four concrete barriers rising up from the asphalt and protecting the front glass doors. Pablo put his truck in reverse and hit the gas.

"Hold on, boys, here we go!" Pablo said to his two partners.

Pablo entered the lot in reverse. Roman drove in on the right by the doors, with Hamms on the left. Pablo jumped the curb and squealed through the lot and smashed through the big plate glass window wall with such force the whole glass wall shattered, from one end to the other. Pablo stopped the truck nearly six feet into the store, and Lowery opened the lid and three flash bangs took flight. Three bright lights then three loud bangs, and Lowery opened the lid again, and he and Brown jumped out of the truck. When

THE DRUG TASK FORCE

Pablo finally got the truck stopped, he was in the second row of groceries. The first row was candies and single-serving bags of chips and dips. In the second row was vehicle maintenance items such as oil, transmission fluid, and windshield wiper fluid. Also little items of tools, oil filters, light bulbs, and tissues, and at the far end of the row were magazines. The second row crashed into the third shelves and knocked over all the canned goods and coffee. Brown and Lowery jumped out of the back of the truck and Pablo jumped out of the cab. Their footing was slippery, and they slide but were able to stay on their feet. As Roman and Humphries came to the front doors they saw two Hispanic males dive over the counter on the West end of the store while Pablo was driving his truck into the store. Roman and Humphries opened fire on the bad guys behind the counter; Hamms and Matt entered along the East wall and encountered one bad guy, in the cooler. The crazy guy was in the cooler looking out when Hamms and Matt put an end to him. Roman and Humphries had one dead guy and one had made it to the back of the store and out the back door. Roman was on the radio to Charlie to let him know he was about to see a man run out the back door when Charlie shot and killed the man trying to escape. The team began to clear the rest of the store and was to enter the office area, when Lowery noticed something. Just as

Humphries was opening the door Lowery yelled out, "trap" and everyone froze just as they were, not another move. Lowery spoke to everyone at the same time and warned them of what he saw.

"Fishing line tied to the door hinges, close the door real easy and everyone back out." Lowery warned in a soft voice.

Everything was dead silent as Humphries was closing the door.

"Easy, easy." Lowery said to Humphries though he did not need to be reminded. The line went limp, the sound of mechanical switches.

"Get down!" Lowery yelled out.

An explosion ripped through the store and glass, pop, beer, milk and anything else back in the freezer and office area went up. The blast luckily was not set up right, it went up and out not out then up. The team starting to recover from the blast got up and began checking themselves for injuries, Humphries still had not moved. Brown and Roman went to Humphries where he was pinned to the ground by the big steel freezer door. Humphries was bleeding from his head but no bad so then Brown and Roman lifted the heavy steel door up and Pablo and Lowery drug Humphries to safety. Humphries began to wake up when Brown placed a cool wet towel on his head wound.

THE DRUG TASK FORCE

"Did I do all this? Humphries said, almost apologetic.

Hamms, with a sigh of relief answered, "As long as you are all right, you owe us for dry cleaning."

The whole team was covered with a variety of foods and drinks.

Pablo found his way to the cooler and the beer and popped a top. "To you. Johnny Walker. He then looked at Hamms. "Give me a break; I just need to get the taste out of my mouth," Pablo said to a watchful Hamms.

Hamms, shaking his head and smiling, got on the radio to the sergeant

"Sergeant, you got a copy? We are all okay."

Sergeant responded, "Roger that. Fire, ambulance, and the bomb squad on their way."

Hamms radioed to Charlie out back for his status. "Charlie, you okay?"

"Ten-four, but bad guy is ten-seven."

"We got three dead bad guys in here," Hamms reported.

"Yes, and all these guys have tats, but still no Warez, though," Roman said.

"Damn, that guy must have nine lives," Hamms said in disbelief.

"Can't have many left," Brown answered

"Gather what you can, and let's cut and run before we find more explosives," Sergeant broke in on the radio.

The team did a quick once over and collected seven more AK-47s and several boxes of ammo and then cleaned themselves up a little bit.

"Let's get out of here. I am tired and sticky," Hamms said as they loaded up.

Chapter 19

Time was 1925 hours

After the team loaded up the evidence and began their drive back to the office, there was some talk on the radio about what had taken place so far during the day.

"Does anybody have any ideas on how this Warez guy keeps getting away?" asked Lowery.

"We were just talking about that ourselves," Hamms followed.

"Two times now, someone leaves just before we get there, and we are ambushed."

"Sergeant, you still on the radio?"

Sergeant answered, "Go ahead."

"Just thinking out loud, can you get a hold of Robert Gates and have him meet us back at the dugout?"

"I will call him in a minute. Right now I have to try to explain this mess to the fire department," the sergeant said in response.

Robert Gates was another older deputy who worked with the Drug Task Force. He was sixty-nine years old and couldn't run or shoot straight, but did have two qualities the team needed, forty years of law enforcement experience and cash. Gates was a very wealthy man who made his money the old fashioned way. He worked two jobs all his adult life. Gates was a business man with his own company, which was a very successful business, and was always buying the team little gadgets for their undercover operations—wireless mikes, surveillance cameras, and even the undercover truck that Brown drove.

Hamms was thinking out loud to all the others on the radio. "We might have a bug in the office. Anyone notice anything different or new?"

"Well, I remember back a couple of months when we tied Brown's shoes to the fan. We had to take them down, because we were getting new fans," Pablo said.

"That's right. When we get back, don't say or do anything in the office until we get this figured out," ordered Hamms.

Hamms immediately got back on the cell phone with the sergeant and began explaining what they were thinking and why he was asking for Gates.

The sergeant then called Gates and told him about their situation, and asked Gates if he had any surveillance equipment or knew where to get some and in a hurry. They needed debugging equipment and items they could use to find listening devises in their office.

Time was 1945 hours

The team waited in the parking lot for the sergeant to arrive, and when he finally got there, they went to

THE DRUG TASK FORCE

the break room, a different area in the sheriff's office, and again waited, this time for Gates, The Gadget Man. Pablo seemed to have a nickname for everyone in the office, and The Gadget Man was Gates.

The break room was a room with chairs, four different vending machines, a TV, and two long folding tables. There was also a kitchen sink with cabinets and a microwave oven. They all were sitting around the tables watching the local channels and getting breaking news updates about what was going on in the city. After the mid-afternoon hanging in the middle of the street, the drive-by shootings, and the police chase with a shootout, the team did not know what to expect. Also with the near riot in the jail and the car fires, the team was not looking forward to nightfall. The sun had long disappeared from the sky, and with the rain clouds and the north wind dominating the outdoor temperatures, the team was anticipating a long, cold night.

Gates finally arrived and had a whole sack full of goodies for the team to try and use. First and foremost for the guys, was the debugging device that looked like the black transistor radios from the 1960s and 1970s. This devise was used for detecting a transmitter or any other low-frequency band. The debugger could cover the dugout and each room in just a couple of sweeps around the room. It would search for any wavelength band and pinpoint its location with a humming noise to indicate the interference. Hamms, the techno geek of the team, took the device and began to read the directions.

Pablo said to Hamms, "Turn the damn thing on and point it just like a gun."

"You are such a redneck hillbilly," Hamms fired back.

"Whoa, whoa, don't get personal; you know my grandpa always said if you need directions to put something together or make it work, you are not smart enough to operate it in the first place."

"That sounds just like something you would say, and coming from you, I believe it."

"I have some listening devices that they told me could hear through walls," Gates advised the team.

"If I get that close to them fuckers, I am going to introduce myself," Humphries said as he took a swallow of his ice cold water.

"Nothing but redneck hillbillies in here," Hamms was quick to reply.

"I have two more of those and some more cameras," Gates said as he unloaded the sack.

"Can someone find me some batteries, and we will see if this damn thing works or not," Hamms said to Pablo.

Pablo hustled back to his desk and gathered up two packs of AA batteries and returned them to Hamms.

THE DRUG TASK FORCE

"Let's go check this out. When we get in the room, carry on like normal, just in case someone is listening," Hamms instructed everyone.

They entered the dugout and the bullpen and then the batting cage. They all had different things to say about Warez, and none of it good. Roman was even cussing the man, and Roman did not use many cuss words. Wayne and the doctor watched as the guys were trying to act normal, but it looked and sounded more like a bunch of grade school kids who were just learning how to cuss. Still puzzled by the actions of the team, Doc looked at Wayne and Wayne back at Doc who asked, "Wayne, have your guys gotten into some of the evidence maybe?"

"Hell if I know. Let's go and see what the hell is going on," Wayne said as they headed into the bullpen.

They left the training room and entered the bullpen where the rest of them were, and they were really confused now. No one was talking to anyone, just six men walking around and cussing at nobody. Hamms stopped in the middle of the room and a little red flashing light came on, and then Hamms pointed the debugger in different directions, to see where the flashing light would speed up or slow down. Hamms pointed the debugger up at one of the ceiling fans, and the light stopped flashing and stayed on, and the machine made a faint beeping noise. Wayne and Doc now figured out what had gotten into the guys, but still did not know why they were cussing at each other. Hamms pointed to the fan and began search his again. After the bullpen was searched, he went into the batting cage, and again the light came on then went solid with a beep, this time to the cork board by Pablo's desk.

"Well, that figures, since I am the brains in this office," Pablo said in a whisper.

Only one device was in each of the rooms, one in the bathroom, and one in the elevator, four altogether. Everyone went back into the break room, and it was clear, so there they had to decide what to do next.

"I hope no one in the office said where they were taking our families while they were in the elevator," Brown said as they entered the break room.

"We better take these things out now or post signs about them all over the place," said Sergeant to the room.

The evening shift captain was called and informed about what had been discovered, and he in turn called the evening sergeant and a deputy to come to the office and take over the sweeping operation and check the entire building.

"The debugger directions said it would also find cameras, but I did not see any of those," Hamms informed the sergeant

THE DRUG TASK FORCE

"Okay, now let's go clear the office, and I don't care if they know we found their ears."

"When we get back, find me the numbers from the first bug and let me get online. I want to see what kind of range these things have; they will have to have a receiver or repeater close by, just like we do with our operations," Hamms said as he began to take charge of the next operation.

Pablo volunteered, "Good, when you find out, me and Roman will go for a walk and see what we can find."

"Better than that, I think Brown, Lowery, and Humpme will walk also."

"I need the walk, for a cigarette break. All this debugging is wearing me thin, and speaking of cigarettes, I need to get some more. I am almost out."

"You should have gotten some at the store, with your beer," Brown said as he started to laugh.

"Now you remind me, and besides, I got distracted when Humpme gave me a Pepsi and milk shower," Pablo said in jest.

"You are welcome," Humphries said in reply to Pablo's crack.

"Let's get 'er done. Oh hell, now I am a redneck hillbilly. Damn you, Pablo," Hamms said as he realized that the joke was on him.

They went first to the bathroom and found the bug underneath the lip of the sink. Lowery copied the make and serial numbers for Hamms, who took them to his desk ,where he went online and discovered that the bugs were real expensive and had a 500 to 1,000-yard range and received in real time with recording capabilities. He wrote that information down and gave it to Lowery, and the rest of the guys went back to the break room to plan.

"We found four bugs, but I bet they do not have four vehicles around here listening to us, so let's plan on finding two vehicles, say big trucks or vans, and remember, they have to be big enough for lots of equipment and at least two people," Hamms said to the team.

"Okay. I have another plan. We can split up in two three-man teams with Humpme, Hamms, and me, then Roman, Brown, and Lowery. We can cover two blocks north and west, and the others will cover south and east," Pablo said.

"We are all SWAT trained, so tactically we will treat it like a vehicle assault with armed and dangerous," Brown reported.

"We have darkness on our side, and they do not know that we know. I will go tell Hamms and put the plan on paper for Sergeant," Pablo stated before he left the room for his desk.

THE DRUG TASK FORCE

Pablo told Hamms that he would write down a quick version of the plan for him and Sergeant Davis. Hamms let the sergeant know about the plan and told him to carry on with Doc and Wayne like normal until they heard back from the guys. The team met at the loading dock at the back of the office, grouped up, and headed out in different directions on foot, with each man carrying his own backpack of equipment. The men also re-attached their new silencers on their Glocks as they separated and left the safety of the sheriff's office for the dangerous and unpredictable streets.

Chapter 20

Time was 2100 hours

On the local news, the weatherman stated that the temperature was forty degrees and falling fast, with no wind and a low ceiling of clouds. The humidity was high and the cold air was thick, which was causing a fog to develop, and with the damp streets, it was a creepy silent on the streets that night. The streetlights were on, and from a distance, there was a halo around the lights that seemed to consume all the light and left only a dim glow that reached the ground. The sheriff's office was located in the northwest corner of downtown, more industrial and entertainment than business or eatery. To the north was a homeless center and the county jail, and west was a wrecker service and railroad yard. To the south was the Federal Building, post office, and a 15,000-seat entertainment and sport center, and to the east were several empty warehouses and, at that time of night, empty parking lots.

There were no sporting events or concerts going on at the Hall, so there was not a lot of activity on the streets. Hamms, Humphries, and Pablo headed west on first street, looking for anything parked along the streets or in the parking lot surrounding the Hall.

THE DRUG TASK FORCE

Several cars, trucks, vans, and big rigs were inside the secured parking lot of the Hall. The men slipped inside the fence and checked all that were there. The lot was secured by an eight-foot-high metal fence with several gates, but with a homeless shelter just one block away, many holes had been made into the lot. The homeless had made their way into the lot for shelter from the winter cold and summer heat, not to cause trouble, and had yet to become too big a problem to require mending the fences. As the trio reached the next corner, they noticed a light-colored Dodge mini van parked on the west side of the street facing their way.

"Hold up and look at that glow coming from the driver's-side window. It takes a smoker to find one," Pablo said as he held up one closed fist as a sign for the others to halt.

A quick glow showed up in the darkness and then disappeared just as fast.

"The driver is smoking, and I bet his window is cracked, too," Pablo continued.

The car was parked on the west side of the street facing south, and only one other car was parked on the other curb, facing the opposite direction. Humphries radioed the other team about what they had found.

"I will tell Sergeant, but we need to make sure we have real bad guys first and not some high school kids smoking weed and getting hummers," Hamms stated.

RUSTY POPE

After the radio traffic, they tried to decide how to approach the vehicle and take down the suspects with the least amount of trouble and keep them from calling their people for help. There were no people on the sidewalk, with only some highway noise that could be heard in the distance. On the west side of the street there was an empty warehouse building with three stories and a small deserted parking lot on the south end of the block. On the north end of the block was a boot and work clothing store that had been in business for over forty years in the same location. On the east side of the road there were two single-story red-brick buildings, and they were part of the wrecker service company, which took up the entire city block. There was an alley that divided the two buildings with no good access to that alleyway.

"You know I got my backpack, which all these homeless people carry, so I will just turn the corner and walk the sidewalk toward the shelter," Pablo explained. It was the first part of his new plan.

"After I pass the van, I will slow down and disappear behind the other car. Then you and Humpme will march down the middle of the street like two old drunk guys, trying to make it to the bridge. Humpme will fall down several times, and you will help him up and work your way to the passenger side. I will then watch the back and the driver," Pablo continued.

THE DRUG TASK FORCE

"I will sling my shotgun around the back and have it at the ready," Humphries said as they prepared for the attack.

"Well, let's go with this plan and see what the fuck happens," Hamms answered as he shrugged his shoulders and began the march down the street.

Pablo went around the corner first, not paying any attention to the van, but from the corner of his eye he can see some movement, but nothing threatening. The men agreed that they would count to one hundred, and then Hamms and Humphries would walk around the corner and make their approach.

At a count of around sixty, Pablo drew even with the front of the van and just a few feet short of the other car. Pablo noticed that beside the driver's side and on the street was a pile of cigarette butts, so the guys had been there for quite some time. Pablo stopped when the count was about ninety, for he had reached the far side of the second vehicle. He checked to make sure it was empty, and then there came the two "drunken" guys staggering down the middle of the street. Humphries began to sing a Hank Junior song and seemed to be a natural at being drunk. Hamms was trying to keep Humphries from falling down, but missed the catch, and down went Humphries.

Pablo, hiding behind the little Toyota car, was enjoying the show, when the driver's side door came open.

Hamms and Humphries continued the act, although they too noticed the door coming open. When they put the plan together, they did not expect the bad guys to come out in the open, and they did not have a plan B. Hamms and Humphries were still twenty-five feet away from the van when a short Hispanic male exited the van.

Pablo had a good look, and the man did not have a gun in his hand as he closed the van door. The two actors continued to act as the man approached them, still with nothing in his hands, but then just fifteen feet apart, things went Wild West. The Hispanic male, short in stature, was wearing a cowboy hat, long coat, blue jeans, and boots. As he approached the two drunks, he reached out and pulled the right side of his coat back, and there in plain view, the man was wearing a holster and gun, Wild West. With only a glow coming from the streetlights and no moon for any extra light, the scene took on the appearance of an Old West shootout at the OK Corral.

Humphries saw the gun first, and while on the ground, yelled "Gun" and rolled to his left and to the curb. Hamms drew his Glock while dropping to one knee. The Hispanic drew, but Humphries and Hamms were quicker and much better shots than the Mexican male, and he was dead and falling backwards before he cleared leather.

THE DRUG TASK FORCE

Pablo, seeing the man fall backwards, began rushing toward the van, and from behind, reached the driver's side door and then fired six rounds through the window. When he opened the door, he saw another Hispanic male bleeding from the chest but still trying to use his cell phone. The man was dressed in blue jeans and a T-shirt and had a blue do-rag on his head. Pablo grinned and said, "Too late for nine one one," and fired one more round. Pablo searched the van while the two drunks dragged the not-so-quick-draw cowboy around to the back of the van and put him inside. Pablo found the cell phone the guy was using, but he did not get all the numbers dialed. The team put both dead men in the back and collected the two receivers and repeaters.

"I hope they did not put two cars on our side, because I am tired and don't want to lug this equipment into another gunfight," Humphries said, huffing and puffing from the heavy loads.

"Me too," Pablo agreed.

"Let's just leave it here and call Sergeant and tell him. Maybe he can get the wrecker company to tow the van with the dead guys inside."

Hamms notified the sergeant and the other team, and the sergeant informed Hamms that he had a plan to get the van and the dead guys off the street.

"I guess this cowboy thought two drunks in the

middle of the night in the middle of the street, he would just have a showdown, and nobody would miss two homeless dudes," Pablo said, shaking his head at the dead Hispanic cowboy.

"I may not look like it, but I watch John Wayne all the time, and I know how to quick draw," Hamms replied, rather proud of himself.

Hamms was bragging all the way back to the office, when they got a call on the radio from the other team. They have spotted two vehicles on the fourth floor of the parking garage to the east of the office. The team had cleared their two blocks when they arrived at the parking garage on the southeast corner directly across the street from the office.

"Now I know why Pablo had us go this way. He remembered this four-story parking lot," Lowery complained as his group continued to walk up four stories of the parking garage.

"Yes, hate to admit it, but he outsmarted us on this one," Roman stated. He too was getting tired.

The team entered through the main entrance, looked around, and saw ten cars still parked on the street-level lot. They approached all ten cars as if expecting each one to be loaded with Hispanic bad guys. All ten cars on the first level were empty. On the second floor there were seven cars, and each of those, too, were empty. The third level had six more

THE DRUG TASK FORCE

cars, but no people. The team was getting tired, and even without any action, they approached every car with deadly force anticipation. When they reached the fourth level, there were only three cars, but two of them were parked next to each other at the northwest corner, which overlooked the sheriff's office. These two vehicles were SUVs, and both seemed to be idling, for exhaust vapors could be seen coming from their tailpipes, although the team could see no lights just a steady stream of steam. At the top level there was no ceiling and no pillars to hide behind, just a wide open parking lot with four tall light poles. These lights were all on. The light bulbs were bright and spread enough light to cover the entire top side, even in the foggy weather. From the street level, with the weather cold and the sky dark and filled with fog, the top floor of the parking garage seemed to be in the clouds. The garage was the tallest structure on this side of town, so the team did not have to worry about lights coming from other buildings or about people watching what was about to happen. The plan was to take out the lights and approach with night vision goggles, identify, and shoot the bad guys.

"Can any of you see in the cars?" Roman asked.

"No, both vehicles are tinted black, so we can't see in, but they will have trouble seeing us after we take out the lights," Lowery answered.

"Get ready to mask up. Lowery and I will take out the lights as we go, and when the lights go out, masks on," Brown told the other two.

"You guys ready to go?" Roman asked.

They started moving.

Lowery and Brown split up and worked their way along the walls to reach the light poles. They took out the first two lights with no apparent reaction from the people inside the SUVs. Roman was approaching from the rear of the vehicle using darkness as his only concealment. Brown and Lowey worked their way to the outer walls of the structure, which were four-foot tall concrete walls. When the men were close enough, they fired again with their Glocks and took out the final two lights on the fourth floor. With everything pitch black, they lowered their goggles and turned on their night vision. With Lowery on the right and Brown on the left side, they were even with the back of the two SUVs and twenty-five feet away. Roman was almost twenty feet back when he saw the back of the left SUV raise the back hatch. He quickly moved to his right just before he saw the first muzzle flash.

Roman moved farther right as he fired his silencer-fitted machine gun into the back of the SUV, and the sound of dull thuds filled the air as he fired one, two, three, four, three-round bursts into the SUV. The door flew all the way open, and he fired more rounds into the back of the SUV. The SUV returned fired, but in no apparent direction.

Brown on the left side with Roman firing watched as the driver's side door opened. The man did not see him, as Brown closed the man's eyes forever with one clean shot to the head.

Lowery still not engaged, had the passenger back and front doors covered and watched as two men tried to sneak out of the car. Lowery had not been seen and waited for the two men to give him a clean shot, and just as they did, Lowery closed them out as well.

Lowery, Brown, and Roman hurried around the two vehicles, stashed the bodies back inside the SUVs, and collected the evidence. The other SUV was empty of men and equipment, so it appeared that the men were getting ready to change places with a new team to take over the watch. Brown let the other team members and the sergeant know what had taken place and where the tow trucks were needed.

Sergeant Davis let the teams know that wreckers were on the way and to be prepared for good and bad news upon their return to the dugout.

Chapter 21

Back in the bullpen, Sergeant Davis, Wayne, and Dan Workman, the ATF agent, were working the computer and phones at the jailhouse. They had to find out how the bugs got into the secured facility and this deep into the Drug Task Force. Sergeant Davis called the captain of the evening shift at the jail to get a list of the trustees assigned to the sheriff's office for the past two months. Sergeant Davis then asked if any on the list were Hispanic males who were serving time for possession with intent to deliver ice, old school meth, or weed, and then if any had tattoos of seventy-seven on their bodies.

The evening shift captain called Sergeant Davis back within ten minutes with the news. There were two men who fit that description, but as of 1500 hours this date, those two men were killed in the riots that had taken place at the jail. Both men were killed by other inmates and not by any deputies working to quell the deadly disturbance that was taking place. The captain informed Davis that six inmates were killed, and they were still counting the injured. He also reported that one deputy was killed and three others injured, with one of those in jeopardy of losing his life.

THE DRUG TASK FORCE

Sergeant Davis slammed the phone down in frustration and then regained his composure and told the rest of the guys the new information. Wayne and Doc walked back in the bullpen, where the sergeant was still talking about what had happened at the jail.

"Sergeant, I took Doc over to the quartermaster office and got him some clean clothes and a shower. I was sick and tired of smelling the blood that was soaked in his clothes," Wayne informed the sergeant

Sergeant Davis and the rest of the guys agreed that was a good idea, because they were getting sick of the smell also.

The doctor, now dressed in class B 511 khaki pants and a tan Polo shirt said he felt much better in the clean clothes and was eager to get back to work.

"Doc and I made a list of places where Warez might be," Wayne told the sergeant

The sergeant took the list and asked the men to explain.

"Well, one address, the house to the south, is still a prime target, but I found something in book two that really got my attention," Wayne explained.

The doctor had walked back to the other office to get the four books returned and handed them to Wayne.

Wayne continued, "Book two mentioned a warehouse on page number ... let me see here." He shuffled through the book.

"Not listed here on this list in your notes," the sergeant stated as he too was looking.

"Okay, let's see."

He was flipping through the pages and then stopped abruptly. "What the hell? There are several pages missing. Doc, hand me the other books," Wayne said as panic started to take over his emotions.

The doctor handed Wayne the other three books, and then the two teams came bursting through the dugout door. "Mission accomplished; four receivers, four repeaters, and six more dead bad guys," Hamms stated like a proud father.

"All in a day's work, Sergeant," Brown added in the same manner.

The boys were full of themselves and relieved that things went well, but the news that the sergeant gave them and the panicked look on Wayne's face brought them back down to earth. Wayne was still upset that he could not find the page that talked about a warehouse and loading docks that Warez had set up, when he stopped, took a deep breath, and looked over at the doctor. In fact Wayne was becoming more concerned, because now he noticed two or three more pages were missing from a couple of the books, and very important pages as well. He knew that no one except for maybe the doctor and himself had been alone with the books since they first came into the office.

THE DRUG TASK FORCE

Dan Workman, the ATF agent, was a medium-height man, thirty-four years old, and had been with the ATF for four years now and was tracking the serial numbers of the recovered AKs. Some of the guns had a very colorful past, from the Middle East, Mexico, and even Canada. What was troubling Workman was that several of the guns were supposed to be in Chicago and ready to be melted into paperweights. Workman was yelling on the phone to someone in D.C., and he wanted some answers.

"Damn it, sir, I need to know about these damn guns. They are killing people, while you are jerking me off on the phone right now. Tomorrow afternoon I will be in your office sticking these guns deep in your ass if I don't get the right answers by the morning. Good-bye, sir." Workman slammed the phone down and kicked the trash can across the room. "Man, I hope my boss does not take that phone call personal, or I will need an application," Workman said to the sergeant who was staring at him in amazement.

"You know he is on the phone right now saying the same thing as you did, only to someone else," the sergeant said, trying to calm down Workman.

Lowery, hearing the anger in the voice of Workman, smarted off, "Truck driving school is taking applications."

RUSTY POPE

The FBI guys were also working the phones and having the same luck as Workman, so there was no real progress made with the phones or computers.

"Hey, guys, I need you to listen up. The streets are still under attack, and more patrol cars have been shot at, but none of our people have been hurt. We discovered that there have been two inmates working in here during the past two months that fit the descriptions of Warez's men, but they have been killed in the jail by other inmates. Now things are starting to slow down, and Walker does not have to have any more surgeries. He is in recovery as we speak. They just released Organ, and he is on his way home. Speaking of home, our families are safe. They have eaten dinner and are expecting a phone call from you guys. So it is now twenty-one forty-five. Let's meet back here at twenty-two fifteen and get ready to grab some more bad guys," the sergeant told the guys.

With that the guys slipped off to different corners and got on the phone to their loved ones. Things were all of a sudden quiet and peaceful and very relaxing, but the guys seemed to know that the time would end soon enough.

Pablo, walking back to his own corner of the office with his head down, was wondering whether he should he call Karen or not. If he did, would it lead to another argument over the phone, or would it be a

THE DRUG TASK FORCE

tender conversation that he so desperately needed at the time?. In either case it could be his last visit with his wife, either by phone or in person, because his time could be short-lived. He decided to make the call and take a chance, for he needed to hear her voice, even if in anger or disappointment. For the last two and half years, Karen had accused him of becoming a make-believe character, Pablo, and leaving Sonny, the man she married, out in the garage. Pablo realized she was right, for it had been a long time since the two of them had spent any time together, emotionally or physically, and it was taking its toll. Back at his desk, he dialed the numbers one at a time, thinking between each number, but at last her phone began to ring. Karen answered in a nice whispering voice, the kind that made Pablo or Sonny melt in her presence.

"Hey, honey, are you okay?" Pablo asked in a low voice.

"Me, I am fine, but I am worried about you."

"No, don't worry about me. I am well, but we still haven't caught up with all the bad guys."

"I don't want to hear about any bad guys or drugs or informants. I am sick and tired of hearing about that. That is all you talk about anymore, this dope bust or that informant telling you lies." Karen's voice had gone from the whispering sultry voice to a sharp and condemning one in just a few seconds, just what Pablo was dreading the whole time he was debating with himself about whether to make the call.

"Wait a minute. This is not my fault, I did not start this killing spree." He took a deep breath and tried to carry on a normal conversation with his wife and he continued. "Honey, what I mean to say is it will all be over soon and—"

She cut him off in mid-sentence. "Listen, Sonny or Pablo or whoever you are right now, I would like for you to return my husband to me, the one I married who was around and showed me and our family that we are number one in his life, not his job, criminals, dope, informants, or other women in the middle of the night. The one that would make love to me and not just go through the motions hoping I would not notice. I do notice, and I don't like the man you have become."

Pablo knew she was right, but he could not afford to lose focus, not now, when so many lives were at stake, but what could he say in his own defense? For the past two years, Pablo had taken over the life of Sonny, and now it was time for Sonny to step up and regain his life. He knew this fact, for even the guys on the team had told him to take some time off and enjoy a weekend, but he couldn't or wouldn't, because for the past two and a half years, Sonny was reborn with a new kind of spirit, a new life full of suspense and thrills that life as a patrol officer did not realize. He

THE DRUG TASK FORCE

was living a life of danger and mystery that had consumed him like a drug. Sonny was the husband, father, and lover, but Pablo did not know how, for he was a junkie, an action junkie.

"I hear you, but let me get through this, and we will talk," Pablo said, desperately trying to save the conversation and his marriage.

"I have heard this song and seen this dance before. I've got to go." Karen paused for a second and then added, "But be careful. I love you."

She hung up the phone before Pablo could answer, but he did anyway, with a choking, "I love you too."

Wayne was busy tearing up his desk area trying to find a few loose pages, very important pages, in Wayne's opinion, but during all that was going on, he too noticed the quiet that had surrounded him and filled the office. He took a minute, poured a cup of coffee, took it to Pablo, tapped him on the shoulder, and handed him the hot cup of coffee. Pablo reached up and took the cup and looked up at Wayne, and with a tear in his eye, winked, smiled, and mouthed the words "Thank you." Wayne smiled back, took a deep breath, walked back to his desk, and started throwing things around again, just like before. Soon Wayne remembered writing the address down and looking it up on the computer. He then looked at the terminal, and it was black. Somehow someone had turned off his computer, which made him angry and upset all over again. All of a sudden he remembered where the address was written, and Wayne had finally found the missing address, after an hour of looking.

"Sergeant, I finally found the address. As soon as my computer is up, I will have it ready for you," Wayne said with relief in his voice.

"Okay, just let me know."

Time was 2220 hours

"Sergeant, here it is. It is a warehouse on East Louisville, and it looks like a twenty-thousand-square-foot warehouse with a couple of loading docks. I looked up the utilities, and the building is owned and bills are paid through an offshore account registered in—get this—Mexico. The utilities are high, so the building is in use day and night," Wayne stated in a triumphant voice.

"Good work, Wayne, now give me an address, and I will send someone to sit on it till we are ready, and I will also call the judge. I hope he is not sleeping too soundly tonight," the sergeant stated with a sense of urgency.

The guys wandered back into the bullpen one at a time after they talked to their families. Some were still a little teary eyed, but a renewed determination was written all over their faces.

THE DRUG TASK FORCE

Humphries was the first to enter. He grabbed a slice of cold pizza and took a seat next to Brown, who had just hung up from speaking with his wife. Humphries looked over at Brown and said, "Ready for this?"

Brown replied, "Ready or not, they left us with no choice."

They did a fist bump and then Pablo entered the room. Pablo, still trying to make the change from Sonny back into Pablo, was having trouble, for he felt like a man with two personalities. He was trapped in between, and he needed Pablo to come back, because Sonny cared too much for the people around him. He needed to be ruthless again with only two things to think about, killing Warez and protecting his team members. After a few taps on his computer keyboard, he got up from his desk and went to the other room. "Another One Bites The Dust" played in the back ground on Pablo's computer. He had reapplied his eye black from this morning, but he had added a two-inch triangle below each eye. Pablo was back and in rare form.

"Choctaw war paint; I'm not a code talker but a scalp taker," Pablo announced with pride in his voice.

"You are so full of shit, no wonder your eyes are brown," Brown answered.

RUSTY POPE

As the rest of the boys entered the bullpen, you could see a new life, a more energized group of men than just a few minutes before. They all seemed to regain their confidence and their own mannerism after their own phone calls to their loved ones. It was like a new day in the office.

Pablo had a lot to do with that attitude, for he was doing a little Indian shuffle, as he called it, not an Indian dance, but a moccasin two-step.

Chapter 22

The time was 2230 hours, and everyone was sitting and discussing the next raid plan, the raid on the warehouse. Everyone was in the room except for Doc, who was in the outer office by himself. Wayne noticed that Doc was not in attendance. With the team already in the bullpen, Hamms began drawing the diagram of the warehouse on the white board with black dry-erase markers, using red for the doors.

Hamms looked at Pablo and said, "No Shock and Awe this time, Pablo. We are going to need stealth, timing, and patience on this one. Anyone who has any ideas, please speak up."

"Do we have any clue as to how many bad guys in the warehouse?" Roman spoke first.

"No, all we know is at least two outside patrols. The unmarked says they are armed with some kind of rifle and side arm. There are two loading docks, with one driveway leading into the warehouse, one door on the north side, one on the south side, and a fire escape ladder to the roof, which has a door. The building is two stories, with several windows on all sides, though they appear to be blacked out, and the second floor is a partial floor, As of right now, both docks are occupied, and there appears to be people inside, maybe getting ready to load up two semis." Hamms continued to draw on the board.

"There, it looks like a tall chain link fence around the place," Lowery mentioned when Wayne brought up a satellite view on the computer.

"Google Maps confirms that fence and a guard shack. It also looks like a razor wire on top of the fence. That will slow us down but not stop us."

"We are going to need bolt cutters to get through the fence, so we don't have to bother with that razor wire," Brown chimed in.

Hamms continued giving out the directions. "Sergeant and Gates in the command van will have the north and east corners, and the unmarked will cover the south and west. If we get stopped, crash the fence and save our asses. More units will be in the area. Humpme, Roman, and Matt get the front main gate and the north door. Charlie, Brown and I will take the south door, and Pablo, Lowery, and Workman take the roof. Boys, we will be going in quiet, and we will give the roof team a little extra time to get up and in before we breech the north and south doors. Roof team, will take care of anything upstairs and cover us from snipers hiding up high. North team will enter and travel toward the center covering west. We will enter and travel to the center and cover east; that way we can limit our own crossfire. Once inside, go slow, identify, and don't miss. Ten minutes to leave."

With Humphries's and Pablo's desks next to each other, the two men had become good friends, and this was the first time in a while that they had any actual time to talk to each other.

Pablo started, "Humpme, I am sorry for your loss, I don't know how or what to say."

Humphries returned, "Man, don't worry 'bout it. I know what you mean, but damn, those girls had nothing really to do with me. These Cartel guys have really made this shit personal."

"I guess this is the way they run their business down south, but up here you don't fuck with the cops' family, or else. And that is where these bastards are, the or-else part. Brother, let me tell you this is going to get worse before it gets better, so keep low and eyes open, one shot, one kill." Pablo grinned at Humphries and winked.

Humphries returned the look, and they went back to gathering their equipment and preparing for the next assault.

The teams were gathered in the parking lot and checking their equipment and radios. The sergeant was confirming all, when he received a call from the unmarked. Four or five males were starting to load one of the semis parked in the dock, and one new truck

RUSTY POPE

had just driven up the ramp and gone inside the warehouse. Each team was loading and driving through the gate of safety and toward another showdown with the Warez Cartel.

Chapter 23

Time was 2245 hours

The night was still, with no wind and a dense fog forming from the ground up. The temperature was cold, the rain was all but gone, and there was no moon. Each team had its own bolt cutters, and each member had one flash bang and one smoke grenade, just in case. On the way over, the teams paired up and drove separate routes to the rally point. Once there, they set their times and said their prayers and drove blacked out the last three blocks to the target. Upon their arrival to their own spot, they once again checked their times.

The warehouse was located less than a mile south of the main East-West Highway. The warehouse was from east to west and the front was facing north and the fire escape was on the east end of the building. The building was made of brick on the bottom half and pole-barn metal on the top half. It was secured by a ten-foot-high chain link fence with razor wire on top. There was a large parking lot on the north and west sides and two rows of parking on the south with just a drive lane on the east. The only lights that were on were the street corner lights outside the fence. On

RUSTY POPE

the inside only the guard shack, one light over each of the walkway doors, and the loading docks were well lit. The roof team was the first to arrive, and they arrived on foot at the east side fence. They cut their way through the fence and entered the secured area. As they approached they hid while the roving patrol went by, so now they knew they had time to make it to the building safely. The patrol was one Hispanic male on a four-wheeler, and he looked pre-occupied and not paying any attention to anything or anybody. He was just driving.

Pablo was the first to reach and climb up the ladder. On the way over, Pablo, Lowery, and Workman played rock, paper, scissors to see who went first, and as usual Pablo lost. Three-quarters of the way up, Pablo heard Hamms say on the radio that the patrol had doubled back and was almost to the corner. Pablo moved to the inside of the ladder as Lowery and Workman jumped into a dumpster to hide, just as the patrol turned the corner.

Pablo, with his back against the building, was watching through the rungs of the ladder as the patrol slowed the four-wheeler to a stop just at the end of the dumpster. Being about twenty-five to thirty yards from him, Pablo unholstered his Glock and took aim at the Hispanic male. The man got off the four-wheeler and walked behind the dumpster and started peeing.

THE DRUG TASK FORCE

Pablo was trying hard not to laugh out loud as he put his Glock away and the man peed and sang some song in his native tongue.

Lowery and Workman, who had jumped into the dumpster were hoping that there was not much trash and no critters to fight. They heard the four-wheeler slowing down, then stopping, and then they heard someone walking toward them singing. They then heard running water. They both looked at each other and knew what was going on just two feet away from them. They too were biting their lips to keep from laughing, when Workman felt something crawling across his legs. He motioned to Lowery, and Lowry could see two mice running around on Workman's lower legs. Lowery was trying even harder now not to laugh, and when he looked at Workman's face, Workman was a macho policeman, ATF agent, scared of nothing, until it came to mice. Workman's face went pale. He started sweating and breathing heavily, and then the running water quit and the four-wheeler started up and drove off toward the other direction.

Pablo was already starting to move around the ladder when Workman jumped out of the dumpster and began running around flailing his arms in every which way. Lowery climbed out and chased him down and began to get Workman back under control. Workman got on the ladder next and began his climb to the top as

Pablo reached the top and climbed over onto the roof. Within the next minute, all three men had reached the top and radioed back to the other that they were in place and ready to go.

The south team of Hamms, Brown, and Charlie had it easy, as they cut the fence and made their way to the south door. When they arrived, they took out the overhead light and were in total darkness. There were only two vehicles parked on their side of the building.

The north team had to deal with the four-wheeler and the manned guard shack, so they decided to drive up to the main gate and badge their way in, or that was what Humphries said they would do. On their approach with Roman driving, Humphries in the passenger side, and Matt in the bed of the truck, they pulled to a stop in front of the main gate. Roman, who never wore a cap, had put on a ball cap and pulled it down low. The man in the shack opened the door and stepped to the truck. Roman rolled his window down, hung his arm in the opening, and in a low voice said, "*Hola, mi amigo.*"

The man responded "*Qué?*" When he got to the door, Roman, still in his low voice, said, "Sheriff's office, and we have a warrant," then raised his arm, and with the other hand, shot the man right between the eyes. Matt jumped out of the truck and caught the dead man before he fell to the ground.

THE DRUG TASK FORCE

Humphries chuckled. "Damn, Roman, you did not give him a chance to answer."

"You didn't see him. He was shaking his head no," answered Roman.

Matt half carried, half dragged the man back into the guard shack and put him on the stool. Matt positioned him so he sat up and appeared to be alert and on watch.

In the background, they all three heard the four-wheeler approaching and coming fast. Matt stayed in the shack with the dead man. Humphries was already out of the truck and opening the gate. The four-wheeler arrived, and a tall Mexican male got off and started yelling at Humphries. The man looked into the shack and saw that his partner was sitting on the stool and watching, so he became even braver and moved closer to Humphries and continued to yell. As he got close enough to touch Humphries, Humphries turned around quickly and fired two shots straight into the man's heart. The man continued yelling for a few seconds, even after he was dead. Humphries had the gate opened up when he shot the man, so he picked him up and zip tied him to his four-wheeler as Roman drove through the gate.

Matt and Humphries jumped into the bed of the truck, and Roman drove to the front of the building and parked in front of the front door. They too took out the overhead light and relaxed in the darkness. As far as they could tell, no one from the loading docks had noticed what had happened at the front gate. As soon as Roman told everyone that they were now ready, Lowery answered back and told them they were having trouble with the door. He told them the door opened out, so they were still trying to get the door opened.

Hamms started talking on the radio to the roof team. "Hurry up, we don't know if the patrols are supposed to report in at any certain time."

"Another minute, Pablo is working hard," Lowery answered.

Pablo was trying to pry the door open enough, using a small pry bar and his dull-ass knife. The bar was in the gap between the solid steel door and the jamb. and using his knife. Pablo stuck it in the gap and was moving the button away from the hole in the jamb. Quiet was a problem now, for all the scratching of metal and Pablo's cussing, as he was getting frustrated, because the other two teams were in the open and were sitting ducks. One more grunt and cuss word, and Pablo's knife had a good bite on the button, and one more twist and the door popped open.

"About fucking time. Tell them we are in," Pablo said to Lowery with a bit a relief in his voice.

"We are in, but there is a short stairwell going down

from the roof to the second floor. Okay, Workman is down, and now we have the roof and stairwell, so whenever you guys enter, we should be ready, just give us one more minute," Lowery informed the others.

"Okay, Roman, one minute from now, we make our entries, but remember, we are still silent." Hamms made the call.

"Ten-four."

Lowery, Workman, and Pablo were at the stairwell landing, visually checking out their area of responsibility and making plans.

"Do you believe this? Who in the hell would design a second floor like this?" Lowery asked in a state of confusion.

"Damn! Looks like something I would design, a drunk, and he had to be confused. This is something I would design on a late Saturday night," Pablo replied as he, along with Workman, stood still and wondered how they would make a safe and unseen approach.

Workman, with his hands on his hips, said, "This is suicide, but there is no turning back now. Nothing left to do but to do it." At the landing and to the left were the side walls and a three-foot walkway around to the front and it, where the contractor started drinking. At the corner was a twenty-foot bridge that connected the two sides. The bridge was at the corner where the walkway turned left to the offices, and the bridge led to the other side, where another row of offices were. The bridge was also three feet wide and about twenty feet long, with a waist-high railing. Over the railings was a view to the first floor and the rest of the warehouse area.

As the team came closer to the bridge and the corner, they could tell that there were four offices on one side and four on the other side. Now the concern was for the crossing of the bridge with no possible cover or concealment for approaching the other side.

"Okay, let's try this: Workman and I will take these offices, and Pablo, you cover us, somehow," Lowery mentioned, but still not confidently.

"Got it, and don't worry about it, just hurry every chance you get," Pablo said as he tried to find a place to cover his teammates.

"Let's move. The other teams are starting to enter the doors," Workman directed the others.

Pablo stayed at the corner as Lowery and Workman entered the first of four offices. The first office was a twelve-by- twelve square room and had only a desk, chair, and a sofa along one wall, and the back wall was covered with five-drawer metal filing cabinets. The other wall had a door that opened into the next room. The floors were wood with no carpet and only a few things on the walls, one picture, a map of Tulsa, and a map of the United States. No one was in this office,

THE DRUG TASK FORCE

and Workman told Pablo that there was a connecting door, so they would just work their way to the end.

At the door they could hear music playing in the second office, so this time they were positive they would meet with some resistance. This time they were right, and as they entered, there was one Hispanic male who was standing by the window smoking weed. He turned to look at who had just entered his office and was surprised by the two deputies. The man had nothing else in his hands but a joint and a lighter.

"Sit down! Sit down and shut up," shouted Lowery.

The man did just what Lowery ordered, but he sat down on the corner of the desk and close enough to the drawers where he could reach inside.

"No, dumb ass, on the floor, now!" Lowery ordered, but this time he showed him roughly.

The man once again complied with the order and sat on the floor.

They placed the man in flex cuffs and gagged him and put him in the far corner of the office. This was the only office of the four that had anyone inside, so when the two exited the last office, they could see the ground floor and noticed that the bad guys below were running and taking cover. Pablo was covering the east-end offices as one window from the last office on the left shattered and bullets flew out.

Workman took one round in the shoulder and fell against the wooden railing. Lowery reached out and grabbed Workman by his vest and held on to keep him from falling over the railing. Pablo returned fire into the last office, and he kept firing until Lowery had saved Workman from falling over the railing and had pulled him back into the office. Pablo reloaded his Glock and told Lowery to cover him as he ran across the bridge.

When Lowery opened up, Pablo ran across the bridge that seemed like a mile long, when bullets were flying. Once across the bridge, Pablo continued to run, right through the right-end office door. There was no one inside, but he could hear men moving around in the next office.

The roof team was separated, and with one wounded and no one else to help, Pablo shouted for Lowery to make his move. Pablo took a position behind a large metal desk in the corner, where he could give some cover for Lowery. Workman had taken a round in his left shoulder, but the round went clean through, so he told Lowery to move, and he could still fire his weapon from this door. Lowery told Pablo he was ready and would come through the first door and hit the bridge running.

Just as Pablo thought about it, the bad guys in the next room opened fire through the walls, which were just paneling and thin, spraying lead all over the office. It sounded like two AKs at the same time. Pablo got as low and as small as he could behind the desk, and then the shooting stopped and a loud bang went off.

Lowery had made it across the bridge and threw a flash bang through the window of the second office. As soon as the bang went off and the shooting stopped, Pablo jumped up and went out the same door he had just entered and joined Lowery at the two windows of the second office. The two opened fire on two Hispanic males in the second office and did not miss. They stopped firing to look around and heard two more shots, this time behind them. Startled, they turned to look as a man fell over the railing from the last office, and they could hear Workman say, "Just a simple thank-you will do."

Lowery replied, "We are even," as he and Pablo cleared the last two offices on the east side of the second floor. As they were doing this, they could hear the gun battle going on downstairs, so they hurried back to the railing and provided fire cover for the teams below.

After the roof team had secured the roof and the stairwell, Hamms gave the go-ahead for the other teams to enter the warehouse. Hamms, Brown, and Charlie made entry through the south door, and they entered into the break room. Not knowing where or what room they were entering, they were surprised to see a half dozen vending machines and tables and even the cleanliness of the whole area. No one was taking a break at that time, so they moved to the outer door of the break room and got ready for another entry. This time they entered in a big open space with nowhere to hide or take to cover if they began to receive fire. The area was open all away across to the north wall. On the right side, or east wall, were four offices that covered the entire length of the wall. To the left, or toward the west, was one semi-truck and lots of toolboxes on wheels. The area looked like the inside of a car repair shop. There was one wall from the north to the south, but it went only half the way. There was another short wall on their side. and these walls broke the warehouse into two halves. The area was so open they could see Roman and his team as they entered into the warehouse.

Hamms looked up, but from where they were, they could not see the roof team or even what it looked like upstairs. Hamms told Roman to move to the semi and to the loading area and that his team would clear the offices. Just like upstairs, the offices all had two windows, with one on each side of the entry door. They approached the first right-side office and made entry. This office, unlike upstairs, was very nice, with a brownish carpet, nicely painted walls, wooden file cabinets, and a big expensive wooden desk facing one

THE DRUG TASK FORCE

of the windows. There was a computer on the desk with a very big monitor and an adding machine and a clock. On the walls hung two maps, one of Tulsa and one of the United States. These maps, though, were different, for they were clearly marked with routes of highways and important small towns all the way from Mexico to Chicago. Tulsa was circled with an X on the inside of the circle. Who knew what that meant?

They moved to the connecting door and made entry into the second office, which looked more like a bedroom. There were folding cots wall to wall in this room. They carefully moved through the clutter and entered the next office, which was just as plush and nice as the first office. The only difference was there were no maps, just clipboards hanging from nails in the wall. As they moved to the fourth and final office, they heard the sound of AK fire coming from upstairs. They burst through the fourth door, and there they ran into trouble, trouble in the form of two Hispanic males who were trying to get their pants on and load their AKs at the same time. This office was also a bedroom, but with only six cots on the floor.

The two men were told to stop what they were doing, but neither did, and they tried to point their weapons at Hamms and his team. The two men tried, but that was all they accomplished before Hamms, Brown, and Bright put them both back to sleep. They checked the other cots, and just before they were exiting the room, they heard the sound of AK gunfire from upstairs, and not just as few rounds but hundreds, and then the sound of a flash bang and then silence.

Brown smiled. "I know they are good, I just hope they are real good right now," Brown stated with a little hope.

"They are, and they are good under pressure. Come on, we got more work to do," Hamms responded.

When they peeked out the door, they saw one male fall from the upstairs, and when he hit the concrete floor, the body bounced once and then settled and the boys could tell it was not one of the roof team. From the doorway they could hear Workman ask for a thank you a then Hamms, Brown, and Charlie got ready to exit the last bedroom office, but this time a bad guy was ready. Bright, the last to leave the office, was nearly cut in half by an AK at close range. Hamms and Brown dove for cover behind some heavy-duty toolboxes on wheels. The assailant was behind a large metal desk and filing cabinets in the corner and apparently had plenty of bullets, because he kept firing and Hamms and Brown could do nothing but stay low. When the firing stopped, they made their move by rolling their big metal toolboxes toward the desk. The bad guy had reloaded, for he began to fire again almost immediately. Brown, with his toolbox, went around toward the left, hoping to get an angle on the bad guy. When he finally got there, he did have a shot, but he needed more, for all he could see was the feet of a man on his knees behind the desk. Hamms and his toolbox were receiving most of the gunfire, when Brown opened up with his nine millimeter ump on the ankles of the bad guy. Brown shot the feet off the bad guy, who yelled out in pain and began to crawl out from behind the desk, and Brown finished him off.

Hamms rushed to Charlie Bright, and Brown joined him there, and they both knew that there would be no saving Charlie. They pulled and carried Charlie's half-torn body into the bedroom and placed him on one of the cots and once again checked for a pulse, but found nothing.

After Roman, Humphries, and Matt had entered the warehouse, they broke off and went toward the center and the far end, to where the semi and trailer were parked. The center walls were actually center partitions that could be slid open and closed. This night the center partition was slid open, which left a twenty-foot gap in the wall. Inside that half of the garage, the men saw a semi parked over an oil pit in the middle of the room. Along the back wall was a large office, and next to it were rows of shelves in which the mechanics had their supplies of tools and parts all stacked neatly on the shelves. On the far wall were large tools, such as air compressors, a mig-welder, cutting torches, and workbenches secured to the wall. There were also two mobile motor-puller A-frames with chains hanging and hydraulic floor jacks, a real nice setup for an auto mechanic business. Above the semi, in the center of the ceiling, was an overhead crane for pulling engines from the big rigs, and there was one engine hanging from the crane.

As the team members were surveying the garage, they could hear mechanics at work and a forklift moving around, when gunfire broke out behind them. Humphries turned around toward the gunfire to cover the team's backside.

The men on the other side could not or just did not hear what was going on in the other half of the warehouse. Matt quickly moved across the opening to the back wall, so the team had some control of the other room.

Humphries saw the ambush and death of Bright and then observed Brown finish off the bad guy. Humphries relayed the information to Roman and Matt, and he saw Matt lower his head. Matt and Charlie Bright had been partners in the Tulsa office for several years, and their children were close in age, so they had a lot in common.

Matt looked back toward Humphries and raised his hands palm up, as if to ask what happened. Humphries told him what he had just seen and that Charlie had no chance. Again Matt lowered his head, and Humphries worried about what Matt would do.

Humphries said to Matt, "Remember, we've got to finish this job. Come on, Matt."

Roman got Matt's attention back by asking for a count of bad guys in the garage area, and as far as both guys could count, they counted five men, two in the trailer, one in the oil pit, one of the forklift, and one Hispanic male standing in front of the office door. Roman, taking charge of his team, told them, "We now know that Hamms and Brown are secure behind us, so now we need to take this garage."

"I will stay along the back wall and get the man at the office," Matt confirmed as he readied himself for business.

"Humpme and I will move to the truck and get the oil guy first," Roman said over the radio.

"Ready when you guys are," Matt replied.

Roman, sensing something, took a second and told Matt, "Matt, sorry about Charlie."

"Right now we've got a job to finish," Matt growled with a new determination in his voice.

From the angles that Matt and Roman had, they could cover the entire garage area, and Roman also noticed that he could see the upstairs offices and walkway.

"Hey, Lowery, can you guys upstairs cover us as we make our way in the garage?" Roman asked on the radio.

"Pablo and I can. Workman is hit, but we got him patched up. and he is okay for now," Lowery answered.

"Let us know when you are ready."

"If you are waiting for us, you are backing up," Pablo answered this time.

The garage area was very clean, with nothing looking out of place. The semi and trailer were parked inside with the engine hood open. It was parked over the oil pit, which was four feet wide, and they were usually six feet deep and fifteen feet long, with one bad guy changing the oil.

As they made their move, the forklift drove back into the garage and toward the back wall. It drove to a wooden pallet, and with the forks down, it raised the pallet off the ground and headed back outside. The men made their move, with Matt along the back wall and then to the office and the one Hispanic male at the door. Roman and Humphries made their way to the semi and the oil pit. Just halfway there, the oil pit man climbed down and out of the engine and spotted Roman and Humphries charging his way. He jumped off the ladder and disappeared in the pit. Roman and Humphries both saw the man disappear in the pit, and with the man gone, so was their element of surprise.

THE DRUG TASK FORCE

Both of the rigs doors were open, so when Roman got to the cab, he climbed inside and looked in the sleeper and found no one. Back in the front seat, just as he was about to go out the passenger side door, another mechanic bad guy rose up and surprised him. He was on a ladder working on the engine on the opposite side of the truck. He was unaccounted for, and another obstacle to the safety of the team. He looked at Roman and Roman at him at the same time, and both men were startled and both ducked for cover. Now this was two bad guys that were hiding and getting ready for an attack.

Humphries did a baseball slide on the clean concrete floor just under Roman's heels as Roman jumped into the cab of the big rig. Humphries peeked over the edge of the pit, but saw no one at the far end but noticed a light at the other closer end of the pit. He told Roman that the pit did not end but went underground to who knew where, but Roman does not answer. Humphries could only hear Roman grunt and cuss as he and the mechanic saw each other at the same time.

"Humpme got one under the hood," Roman yelled to Humphries.

Humphries yelled back, "Got one underground. I'm goin' in the pit."

Just then Humphries could see the mechanic jump from the ladder to the ground and run for the outer doors. Humphries yelled to Roman, "Got a runner toward the door."

Roman leaned out of the cab and shot the mechanic just before he reached the outside overhead doors. Roman stepped out of the cab of the truck and was in a hurry to reach the dead mechanic and pull him back and out of sight. As he was moving away, he heard a door slam behind him, loud Spanish words, three quick dull thuds, and then no more Spanish. Matt, who had worked his way to the front of the office, was surprised by the Hispanic male who opened the office door right beside him. The male did not see Matt, as he was focused on Roman and aiming his shotgun at him. Matt fired one round into the backside of the man as two more rounds were fired from upstairs. Roman had stopped for just a second, until he heard the three thuds, then he continued on his mission to hide the dead mechanic. As he began to pull the dead man away from the door, the forklift made another appearance. This time the forklift was loaded with a wooden pallet full of something wrapped tight in cellophane wrapping, and the lift was coming in fast. Roman slid the dead man behind the rear dual tires and dived to cover behind the same tires. The driver of the lift was not in the seat but on the far side of the lift as if riding a horse sidesaddle. When it got far enough into the garage, the driver caught a glimpse of Roman diving for cover, and he opened up on the back tires with a fully loaded automatic AK-47. The driver was using the pallet for cover from the front, and he did not slow down. He drove past the back of the truck and was heading straight for Matt and the front of the office.

Humphries, seeing this, was now in the line of fire, as the driver was spraying lead all the length of the trailer and cab, so Humphries reluctantly jumped into the oil pit. Roman or Matt from their vantage points had no shot at the sidesaddle driver, so called for Pablo and Lowery. Just as he started speaking, the upstairs cover started firing on the forklift. Pablo and Lowery did not have a clear shot but sent a lot of lead toward the fast-moving lift.

The lift, without a driver steering it, ran over the Mexican male who ran out of the office earlier, and when it ran over him, it tipped to and fro, causing the rider to lose balance and fall off, providing Lowery and Pablo a clean shot, which they took advantage of and ended this threat.

Two more men on foot came charging through the same door just behind the forklift and started firing upstairs at Lowery and Pablo.

Humphries from the front end of the pit rose up with his shotgun and blasted the first one, the one on the right, and Roman, now not taking fire, rolled to his right and finished the second attacker. Matt, having dodged the driverless forklift, watched as the lift came to rest with the forks and pallet stuck into the wall of the office. The pallet broke and the packages fell off the lift and the contents spilled out onto the garage floor. The contents mixed with some blood from the driver made a sticky red mess.

Matt ran over to the lift and shut the motor off and then ran and jumped into the pit with Humphries and they started to search for the last bad guy. The pit opened up at that end and into a storeroom that contained all different kinds of oils and sizes of filters. Also there was a ladder stairwell that led up and back and into the garage main floor office. There was a back door in the office which led outside. From the outside there was no way to identify that a door was there, almost a secret passageway for escape. The man was nowhere to be found. Both men looked around outside, but in the darkness and the man had a good head start, so there was no way for the two to locate the escapee. This was bad for the team, for that man could tell Warez and give him a head start for him to leave Tulsa.

Hamms and his team had reached the opening and just watched as Roman and his team cleared the rest of the garage. Hamms then got on the radio to the sergeant to let him know all was clear and the bad news of Charlie and that one of the bad guys got out.

THE DRUG TASK FORCE

Brown and Roman cleared the other two semis that were outside and being loaded, but both trucks were empty of bad guys but full of weed, imported hydroponic weed, the expensive kind. They closed the back of both trailers, and the sergeant in the command van pulled into the lot and beside the loading docks.

"Hey, Sergeant, both trucks full of weed," Brown told the sergeant.

"I have got people on the way to secure the warehouse and all within. Also have EMSA and fire in route," the sergeant stated as he took a tour of the garage and goods that would soon be confiscated.

"Hope they have a truck. I bet we got almost a dozen dead bad guys and Charlie and Workman," Roman said, shaking his head in disbelief as to what had just taken place.

"I got one EMSA for our guys and one for them," the sergeant answered in a mellow tone.

Pablo and Lowery, helping Workman, had just now made it downstairs, with the first stop being the room with Charlie. There they paid their respects to a man they had grown to admire and respect. There they met up with Hamms and Matt, who were taking this pretty hard. Charlie was a tough cop on duty but a gentle-hearted man off duty, who was a devoted husband and father to two young children.

RUSTY POPE

An ambulance arrived and took Charlie and Dan Workman to the hospital, and Matt followed in another truck. The team secured the building after the last truck had left with the rest of the bodies. The team did not worry too much for the evidence, since the building was locked and deputies and TPD were guarding the outside grounds.

The time was 2355 hours as the paramedics loaded up Workman and Bright. The guys hung around a little while by taking pictures of the maps and collecting all the documents that hung on the clipboard in the main offices. By the time they loaded up, it was 0020 hours.

Hamms rode back with Pablo, and Lowery while Brown rode with Roman and Humphries. Not much talking went on during the twenty-minute drive back to the office.

Chapter 24

After the teams had left for the warehouse, Wayne fixed a new pot of coffee and pulled two chairs up in front of the TV that hung from a wall mount over Walker's desk. Doc joined Wayne as the two watched the 2300 news and monitored the radios. The news said that the local police and sheriff's deputies had started getting more control back on the streets and that the random violence had diminished drastically in the last hours. Doc turned to Wayne. "Your guys are amazing the way they are staying after Warez."

"When he fired the first shots, he started something with the wrong group of men," Wayne stated as he nodded his head.

"In Matamoros, the police would have already quit and gone home to hide."

"These guys are a tight group. They look out for each other, and they know each other's families. That is why they have taken this fight personally. You mess with one, and you mess with all, just the way these guys roll."

"To Warez, it is all a business, and your guys are cutting into his bottom line, his cash flow."

"Well, I guarantee you they will cut into more than his cash flow as soon as they get to him."

"I hope so. In the last year over seven thousand, seven hundred people were killed in Mexico, and just over seven thousand this year. In Matamoros, a smaller city on the border has lost over five hundred people this year alone, and there is still two months left. Warez is in business, and he means business too. He made well over three million dollars every two or three months, especially in the summer months. The police back home can do nothing to control the cartel because they have so many people on the payroll. If anyone stands up to him, he just has them killed and pays someone for the dirty work."

"How can that be? This is twenty ten, not the seventeen hundreds or eighteen hundreds."

"It is the Wild West down South. I have been to one of Warez's super labs to treat him and some of his workers. He has three super labs in the country, and they work twenty-four-seven. They pump out as much as five kilos per hour in each of the three labs. So that is a lot of cash and now there is a problem and the problem is Tulsa Oklahoma.

"Were those times before or after your family was killed by that bastard."

"Before, Warez had a bullet wound in his right foot he got that in a gun battle with the police. And the other time there were two workers, females, trying to smuggle some ice out of the lab. That was ugly and I will not say anything more about that."

"I will not ask."

The two men sat in silence till a commercial came on and Wayne turned the channel to Fox News and Tulsa had made the national news. As the two drank their coffee and watched Fox, Wayne got up and went to his desk and brought back the third and fourth books and began to thumb through them.

"I thought I saw something in book three about Warez having a brother. Do you know anything about a brother." asked Wayne.

Doc then choked on a drink of coffee and complained that it went down the wrong pipe and quickly changed the subject back to the battles in Matamoros. Wayne just nodded but kept on thumbing through and reading in book three. Wayne stated enthusiastically, "Here it is. My brother the prominent man in town has all the keys to the city." Doc once again changed the subject and started speaking of the three super red phosphorous labs that Warez has in operation. Speaking of how they have developed a recipe to make their own ephedrine and the process of how they turn the powder into ice. How ice is a slightly lower grade but it is easier to package and they can charge more per gram. Ice is the real money maker for the Cartel. Also he made mentioned of the

10-100 acre fields of marijuana and the different kinds of the weed. Wayne is still reading and trying to find out more about this mysterious brother when the teams arrived back at the office.

The time is 0050 hrs.

Wayne and Doc greeted the men as they entered the office one at a time, Hamms, Lowery then Pablo, it did not take long for Wayne to recognize that something was terribly wrong. Though he did not ask who, he knew the team had lost some of their own, so he quietly waited for the others to return. The first three men all went to their own desks and sat in quiet remorse for their fallen friend and then Brown, Humphries and Roman entered and did the same as the first three men. Wayne now knew that something had gone deadly wrong for Charlie Bright and Dan Workman for those two who did not return. Pablo, Lowery, Hamms, and Brown were covered in blood, and none of the men acted like it was their own blood. Again Wayne poured Pablo a cup of coffee and took it to him and asked him.

Pablo gave him the news as to what had taken place at the warehouse and also reported that Warez, Ramerez, and Cortez were all still alive.

Doc asked Pablo, "At any of these locations, have you guys not seen a slick, blue extended cab Dodge truck?"

THE DRUG TASK FORCE

Pablo answered without looking up, "Check with the sergeant. I have not heard anyone talk of that kind of truck."

Humphries, hearing the conversation, spoke up. "At the house and convenience store, that kind of truck left just before we got there, kind of like they knew we were coming."

"Well, that truck belongs to Warez, and I bet Cortez and Ramerez are with him," informed Doc as he turned to Wayne. "Wayne, if that truck is anywhere around where you guys have been hitting, then Warez and his bunch are there."

"How could that be? I mean how could he know that our guys are hitting these exact locations where he is?" Wayne said.

Doc spoke again. "Money talks, and that is how Warez and the cartel got here and got this operation going."

"Whoa, just a minute here! Don't bring that shit in our house. Money does not talk in our office!" Pablo said as he got up and walked over to the doctor.

"I am not Wayne and not your friend or in a good mood, so do not ever let me hear you imply that kind of bullshit again, not in here, hear me?"

Doc was startled by the sudden outburst from Pablo but answered, "I am sorry, but—"

"But this;" Pablo started, but Humphries, who had already gotten up and was close enough, stopped Pablo just in time.

"Doc, come over here for a minute and take a look at this," Wayne said as an excuse to get Doc a safe distance from Pablo and the rest of the guys. "Doc, let's go in here and ask Hamms about the truck, and I need to give him the map, pictures, and address of the Warez compound."

"Okay, but I need to go to the bathroom first," responded Doc.

Humphries said that he needed to go also, so he went with Doc. Humphries and Doc left and went their way while Wayne and the cooled-down Pablo entered the bullpen to talk with Hamms. Humphries let Doc go first, but he also entered the bathroom and stood by the sink washing his hands and face. "Standard procedure, Doc. I know you have been in here before, but you know how it is. Go ahead, you first."

Doc stood over the bowl for almost three minutes and could not go. He quit trying and moved over for Humphries.

"I guess I can't go with someone standing over me and watching," Doc said as he and Humphries traded places.

In the bullpen, Wayne was explaining to Hamms and the other about the Dodge truck and the new target location. "I will send a team over there right now," Hamms said to Wayne.

Doc and Humphries returned from the bathroom trip and caught the tail end of that conversation, and Doc again spoke up. "No need, the addition was a gated community and secured neighborhood. The guard might alert Warez, you know money talks."

"Give me a few minutes, and I will go and sneak in and get eyes on," Brown said from his desk.

"Good idea, but are you sure?" Hamms said as he turned toward Brown.

"I am sure. I got this," said Brown, who was now standing and looking around for his pack.

"I will go too. Can't send just one man," volunteered Lowery.

"All right, we got time, so get some rest and food and clean up, then go when you are ready. We will make plans and leave as soon as you guys give us the word."

"We will take a short break and then get set up and see what is going on. Maybe we could use those bionic ears that Gates brought in," stated Brown as he started digging around through all the new gear.

Humphries re-entered the bullpen, and this time Doc came all the way in, just a few steps behind Humphries. Pablo walked over to Doc and looked him square in the eyes and apologized for the previous outburst and thanked him for all the help he had given the team, and Wayne and then reached out and shook the man's hand. Then he looked at Wayne and thanked him for cleaning up their office and told Wayne, "Now get Doc the hell out of this office." After they left the office, Pablo turned to the others and said, "I don't care what you guys think of Doc, but he is not all on our side. I don't trust that…that son of a bitch. Not even with Roman's life."

"What did you say?" Roman looked up.

Pablo hurried to the doorway, just in case. The guys took time to reload magazines, flash bangs, and anything else they were running low on. Brown and Lowery opened the bionic ear box and got it ready to go, along with some warmer coats for an extended stay in the cold night air.

Time was 0115 hours

Hamms, on the computer looking at Google Maps, turned to Brown. "Brown, you and Lowey get out of here by oh one forty-five and keep us informed as to what you see and hear."

"Roger that, we will," Brown answered.

The sergeant and Gates were just getting to the office, and Hamms grabbed them and got them caught up with the plan at hand. Hamms also told them about Doc and some uneasy feelings that Pablo and Wayne were starting to have.

THE DRUG TASK FORCE

Humphries got in the conversation also about Doc. "Sergeant, I took Doc to the bathroom, and he did not go. I did, thank you, but it seemed to me that he really wanted to be alone, and maybe not just to pee."

"Get Wayne in here and stay with Doc until he gets back, and don't let on that anything is up," the sergeant said to Humphries.

Wayne came back into the bullpen, and the sergeant and Hamms questioned him more about the actions of Doc. Wayne tried to explain his uneasiness with Doc. "The only thing that bothers me is the missing pages in the ledger and the trouble I had at my desk."

"Be careful, and run him through NCIC just in case," Hamms mentioned.

"Already ran NCIC and Triple I, with negative results."

"That's fine, but don't get too trusting with him," warned the sergeant.

Wayne returned to sit with Doc and again started to talk about the missing brother. Doc did nothing but give vague answers and a lot of "I don't knows." Wayne was starting to get more and more suspicious with every answer.

Hamms spoke jokingly to Brown. "Brown, you and Lowery ready yet, or do you need more time for your makeup? Damn, this is not a date."

Brown replied, "Hell, it is cold outside, and you are sending me with Lowery, Mr. Prude. He is still changing clothes, and I think he is taking some Midol. You know, this is his time of the month."

Lowery groaned in self-defense. "I am ready now, you dick heads. I hate all of you."

They gathered up their equipment and headed for the parking lot and Brown's truck. Once in the lot, they were met by Matt, who was at the hospital with Bright and Workman. Matt told the two about what he had learned at the hospital about Workman. "It does not look good for Workman, and his left arm, he might lose it."

Both Brown and Lowery consoled Matt then told him what was about to happen, so he hurried inside to get his equipment ready and get even with Warez.

Brown and Lowery had changed into black BDU shirt and pants and packed their night vision, flash bangs, green smokes, and the bionic ear. Lowery had his mini 14 and Glock, while this time Brown took the twelve-gauge shotgun and his Glock. Now the two were ready to leave and headed out at 0150 hours.

Back inside, the rest of the team also changed into black BDUs, but they were packing light, with only their Glocks. Matt did load up another twelve-gauge and used a Magic Marker on the five rounds he loaded. He marked all five rounds with "Warez."

THE DRUG TASK FORCE

After twenty minutes, the radio came to life with the sound of Lowery's voice. "We drove by, and sure enough two Hispanic males were at the gate. We went around the corner, and we found a good place to park, one block over, and we're on the move to the fence on the northwest side. Cover is good and no one is outside but us."

Roman, who was the closest to the radio, answered, "Use your head, but get as close as you can, then call back. We are just about ready ourselves."

Pablo took a few extra minutes and sneaked off to the break room and called Karen again, this time with no hesitation and a heart full of hope, but he got no answer, and he left a message.

"Hey, it's me again, Sonny. I will see you soon," he said into the phone. He hung up but was smiling from ear to ear, for he knew he had just made a decision that would bring his love back to him. He returned to being Pablo with a sigh of relief and justice in his heart.

Chapter 25

When Lowery got on the radio, Brown checked the time, which was 0233 hours They made it over the outer fence with relative ease and started making their way through the back yards and side streets on their way to 97012 E. Fairmont Lane. This neighborhood was an exclusive one that people had to be invited and accepted into before they could build and move in. The neighborhood covenants required at least 4,000-square-foot homes with 75% brick and only certain types of fences and backyard sheds allowed. All the vehicles had to be parked in driveways or garages, and all front yards were manicured in the same style. A very nice neighborhood, but all the homes, especially at night, looked the same, which was causing the guys some trouble finding the street names, and some of the house numbers were the same color as the brick or trim they were hanging on. The men finally made their way four blocks deep into the neighborhood and found the right house. The house was bigger than 4,000 square feet, and it was a two-story home with a four-car garage. The house was the third on the block, and the street was a dead end. There were only three houses on each side of the road, and it was this way

THE DRUG TASK FORCE

throughout the entire housing edition. The driveway was on the west side of the house, but the driveway started on the north side and curved around. There was a solar gate across the driveway just off the main road. The fence was a black vinyl chain link with wooden posts and railings that covered the entire lot. The front door was just off the driveway, and by design, the bedrooms or den faced Fairmont Lane. There were four windows and evergreen shrubs along the side of the house facing the street. There was a streetlight at each end of the block, which Lowery took out while they were still getting to the house. The two put on their night-vision goggles, as darkness was in charge of the outer perimeter.

Both guys down on one knee looked toward the house. Brown reported, "Got one camera on each end of the house facing Fairmont."

The men made their way to the west end and the fence when a light came on in the front of the garage doors.

Both men pulled their goggles off, and Lowery said, "Damn, motion light came on. I hate them damn things."

Since the street was a dead end, there was a field farther west, and it was a park with walking trails in and out of a lightly wooded area. Also there was a playground area with swings and other playground equipment. The light could have picked up a rabbit or some other critter of the night, but then a male came out the front door and began looking around. The man looked to be six feet tall with jeans, boots, coat, cowboy hat, and shotgun.

Brown looked at Lowery. "Must be a rough hood inside these gates, if they have to have an armed guard."

Lowery, agreeing with Brown replied, "Fixing to be a lot rougher, especially when Matt gets here."

"I just hope he gets it together before he gets here."

The man came all the way out and turned left and was going to go around the entire house. The left side garage door opened, and parked inside was the tricked-out blue Dodge truck.

Lowery, seeing the truck first, smiled and got on the radio. "Hope you guys at the office can hear me. We have conformation that a blue tricked-out Dodge truck in the garage, so get a move on. Don't want to miss him again."

The man disappeared around the far corner of the house.

Brown, trying to figure out how to approach the house, saw a problem and told Lowery, "Fuck me; there is a sensor alarm on the damn fence. Now what the hell are we to do?"

"Shit, that is going to add a degree a difficulty to our entry."

THE DRUG TASK FORCE

Back at the bullpen, the others were making their final preparations to their gear when they heard Lowery on the radio. The guys were concerned about the cameras and the alarm, but they were pumped up with the news about the truck and Warez.

"Boys, Doc says that is the truck, and if it is there, so is Warez," Wayne said to the group as they make their final preparations.

"We need to leave before Warez tries to get away again," Hamms said as he headed for the parking lot.

With the loss of two more men from the team, Hamms called Jeff Warren to come and help. Warren was on the team when Pablo first came over but was transferred because of family problems. Warren was five feet ten inches tall and a little heavy but a good cop and in his element when it came to the outdoors. Pablo, Warren, and Matt got into Pablo's truck, and Roman and Humphries climbed in with Hamms, while the sergeant and Gates once again drove the command van.

Chapter 26

On the way over, Lowery was giving directions to the other two teams and where they needed to come in from. They were to park on 81st street and come through the park toward the east and find the southwest fence corner. Then one team would go farther east along the fence line to the southeast corner, where the members would make their entry.

The two teams arrived after a twenty-minute drive and a ten-minute hike through the park to their own entry points. Brown had noticed when they came through the additions that there were no dogs in the entire neighborhood. Brown commented to Lowery that was one good rule that had to be part of the housing rules.

The alarm sensor was two wires woven throughout the chain link that covered the entire length of the fence, so the men had to figure a way to go over the fence without setting off the alarm. The alarm would sound if any disturbance occurred with the wire or the fence itself. This was a first-class alarm and no good way to defeat it, especially in the dead of night.

Chapter 27

Back at the dugout, Wayne and Doc were left alone again. Wayne stepped out to go to the bathroom, and on his return, he found Doc in the bullpen staring at the chalkboard as if trying to memorize the details.

"Doc, you know you are not allowed in here, especially by yourself," Wayne reminded Doc, who did not even turn around.

"I was just getting into some of these cheese balls and pretzels. It's been a long time since I have eaten anything. Sorry."

"Well, grab the cans and come back in here. I want you to look at this."

Wayne showed Doc more pages that mentioned Warez and his brother. Wayne also showed him where there was mention of a doctor. Doc assured Wayne that that was two different people. Doc tried to explain who this brother was and who the doctor was and that neither of them was him.

Wayne was starting to get a bad feeling about Doc and his answers to these questions. Wayne sat down at his desk and was reading more in the fourth book, when he heard a humming sound coming from Pablo's desk. The doctor was sitting at Walker's desk watching the TV. Wayne saw Doc reach into his pocket, worm his hand around, and the humming stopped. Wayne went back to reading, but after he had read several more pages, Doc got Wayne's attention.

"Wayne, I am going to the bathroom. Back in a second," Doc said, breaking the silence.

"Wait. I will go with you."

Wayne was putting the ledger down when something caught his attention. "Oh hell, go on by yourself. It is just you and me, and you don't need me to hold your hand."

Doc nodded and went out, but Wayne noticed he had his hand in one of his pockets, the same pocket as before. Once again Wayne overlooked the apparent coincidence.

This time when Doc entered the bathroom by himself, he pulled his hand out of his pocket with a cell phone in hand.

Chapter 28

The outside motion light had just gone off when the man turned his fourth corner and was back to the front door, which caused the motion light to come back on. Lowery looked at Brown and asked, "How long was that light on?"

The garage door began to close, and the man hurried under the closing mechanical door.

Brown whispered, "Ninety seconds. You guys hear that? The light will go out in ninety seconds, and we need to make our move."

The other two teams acknowledged the transmission and prepared to scale the fence. Pablo and Warren got on all fours, and Matt got ready to step on their backs and jump over the fence. All three teams were going to use the same technique to overcome the fence.

The light went out, the first member of each team went over, and then the second. The third would be the challenge. Pablo used his pack as a step and then grabbed a hold of Matt and Warren and flung himself over in a summersault. The landing was bad. Pablo landed flat on his back, which sucked all the air from his body, and he lay there gasping for air. The other two teams made it over without any problems. It took

Pablo a few extra seconds to regain his air. Brown and Lowery, in the front yard and directly in front of the front door, ran up the fence line to the corner of the house, but once again that motion light came on. Hamms, Roman, and Humphries had not made it to the house when the light came on, so they were lit up for a second before they made it to the parked trucks in the driveway. Pablo, Warren, and Matt had no trouble with the light, but they had seen the corner camera move in their direction.

Chapter 29

After Doc had left the room, Wayne looked over at Walker's chair and noticed a small piece of paper on the floor. He retrieved the small folded piece and opened it up and discovered a phone number. He took it back to his desk and sat back down and stared at the number and wondered where it came from.

Doc, in the bathroom, opened up the phone and looked at the text message. "Where are they?" was displayed across the screen. Doc was typing when a knock at the door stopped him.

Surprised, Doc answered, "Hang on, Wayne, I am wiping my ass."

"Open this damn door," shouted Wayne.

Doc finished his text, pushed Send, flushed the toilet, turned off the phone, and closed the toilet lid. He turned on the water as if to wash his hands and climbed on the toilet lid and reached up and stuffed the broken phone in the ceiling tiles and got down, turned the water off, grabbed a paper towel, and opened the door.

Wayne yelled at Doc, "What the hell is this? Whose number is it?" Wayne handed the paper to Doc, who took the note and looked at it and then at Wayne.

"Must have come from one of your guys. I don't recognize the number, and besides, I don't have a phone."

"I got this under your chair after you got up. I cleaned that area, and it was not there before."

"That paper could have come from any one of your guys when they changed clothes."

"Well, maybe. You need to get back in the office."

Wayne noticed the toilet lid closed and saw mud or something on the lid, but made no connection.

On the screen just before the phone went black it displayed the last message "YOUR HOUSE."

Chapter 30

Hamms, Roman, and Humphries made it to the two trucks parked in the driveway, when the front door opened again, and the same man came back outside. This time he had a radio and a shotgun. He left the front door, and this time he pumped a round into the shotgun chamber and listened to the radio. He began a slow and deliberate approach toward the trucks and to the outside of the left truck.

The three deputies had ducked behind the right-side truck and were hiding from the lone shotgun-packing sentry. Hamms whispered, "Damn cameras," more to himself than to anyone else around.

The man left the front door open when he went to check around the trucks. More directions came from his radio, and he stopped, backed up, turned, and went a different direction. The sentry was at the front of the driveway with his back to the garage doors. He walked slowly around the front of the truck the three deputies had hid behind. The left garage door came to life, opened up, and revealed the three men.

Hamms and his team were still hiding when Hamms said, "Shit, we've got to move, and now."

RUSTY POPE

The man made his way around to the front side of the second truck and was about to walk right into the three hiding men. Roman laid down on the driveway and saw the man's boots on the side of the truck only ten feet away. He fired two rounds and hit both of the man's boots, and he fell to his knees. Roman fired two more shots at the man's thighs, and the man fell sideways to the ground. Roman fired two more rounds into the man's chest. The final two rounds finished off the man, but not before he could warn the people inside the house.

Hamms acted quickly, and before Roman had fired the last two shots, dove under the rising garage door when it was only three feet off the ground. The garage door squealed to a stop and then started back down, as the interior door slammed shut. Hamm's could hear someone inside the house locking that door. By himself, he worked his way to the front and punched the button to open both the garage doors.

Brown and Lowery, seeing the man go down, raced to the front door in an attempt to secure a way into the house. Just as they reached the threshold, the solid core door began to close, and Brown, being first, rammed his shoulder into the door, and both men entered the house.

Plaster and wood splinters filled the air, along with the sounds of a twelve-gauge pump shotgun.

THE DRUG TASK FORCE

Not knowing where his men were in the house, Brown entered and continued straight and into a hallway, trying to find a place to hide and regroup. Lowery came in right behind him and was able to return fire and slow down the shotgun blasts. Brown went straight and left in a hallway. To the right were the living room, dining room, and kitchen. Just to the left in the hallway was a door to the first bedroom, which Brown was able to clear by himself.

Lowery was still engaged with a man in the kitchen.

In the first bedroom was a twin bed with a pink decorative bedspread, and on the walls were posters of Justin Beiber and Hanna Montana. The closet was filled with dresses, shoes, and girl's toys. No one was hiding under the bed or in the closet, so Brown left the room undisturbed. Brown moved farther down the hallway to protect Lowery, who was loading a new magazine.

Pablo, Matt, and Warren had made it to the back corner of the house when they first heard the automatic gunfire from inside the house. There were six windows along the backside of the house, and Matt was able to peek through the blinds of the first window and see into the kitchen. "I got one bad guy in the kitchen shooting maybe at the front door, and hard to tell who he is shooting at."

Pablo answered, "Probably one of our guys, so flash bang his ass and take him out and give our guys some help."

Warren, hearing the instructions, said, "I will break and rake the window, and Matt, you can throw the bang."

As soon as Warren raked the broken window, Matt threw the bang, and a second later, a bright flash and a loud bang went off.

Lowery, with a new magazine, had fired one round when he noticed the window break and an object went flying through the air. He expected a loud bang and got it a second later. The bang went off right behind the bad guy, and the man fell to his knees and grabbed his ears in pain. Lowey made him forget the pain in his ears.

Hamms had both garage doors open, and Roman and Humphries for protection began to ram, kick, and shoot at the door, trying to gain entry. Finally the door gave way, and the three made entry into the kitchen. Matt was at the kitchen window, while Pablo and Warren did the break and rake on the remaining five windows. They returned and met with Matt at the back door.

The hallway was decorated with pictures and trophies hanging on the walls. Brown had made his way to the next bedroom when he heard Lowery say that Hamms's team had secured the kitchen and to wait for him. The two made entry into what appeared to

THE DRUG TASK FORCE

be the master bedroom. This room had a king-size knotty-pine country-style bed, two oversized dressers, and a fifty-two-inch TV mounted on the fireplace mantel. There were two twelve-point mule deer heads mounted on the wall and a picture of a beautiful naked woman above the headboard of the bed. The bed was made, but there was a suitcase open on the bed, along with lots of men's clothing in the case and on the bed, some folded neatly and some thrown about.

Brown held the doorway while Lowery cleared the huge walk-in closet that was filled with both men's and women's clothing. Next was the master bath, which was also empty of suspects. Both Lowery and Brown heard noises from upstairs and could tell that people were moving around on the second floor. Pablo told Hamms to let them in the kitchen door.

Now the whole team was in the house, and the first floor was cleared. Matt looked at the dead man in the kitchen and said, "One general down and two to go."

The dead general on the ground was the general of money, Roberto Cortez. As Pablo was hurrying through the dining room, on the table was a cell phone, and it was buzzing with a text message. Pablo looked down at it, and the screen read, "YOUR HOUSE." Pablo picked it up and said, "It is my house now, mother fucker," and put it back on the table.

Chapter 31

Wayne and Doc re-entered the batting cage. Wayne went to his desk and turned and stared at Doc for a few seconds. Wayne was starting to put the pieces in place. His suspicion of Doc grew, and Wayne was now concerned for the safety of the team as well as his own.

Doc, seeing a look of confusion on Wayne's face, was starting to get worried himself. Doc then said, "Wayne, you okay? You are staring at me and making me uncomfortable."

Wayne, getting caught, smiled and answered, "Oh no, my train of thought went blank. Grab some change from Walker's desk and get us something to drink."

"Sure, back in a minute."

When Doc opened Walker's change drawer, he spied a black three-inch folding Geber military commando-style knife. He rifled through the change, trying to find two dollars' worth of quarters, and picked up the knife as well. Doc turned and asked what kind of pop that Wayne wanted and then left the office for the break room.

Wayne, having just a few minutes, went to his desk, opened up the fourth ledger again, and began turning pages toward the back, and there he finally found the

THE DRUG TASK FORCE

last piece, William Warez, the prominent Dr. William Warez, from Matamoros, Mexico. He was the family's good son, who turned bad when the Mexican State Police raided his family's home looking for Edwardo Warez. During the raid his family was killed. He was not at home at the time; he was making a house call and delivering a baby on the other side of town. Wayne now realized why Edwardo kept leaving the target houses just in time, but how did Doc get the warnings out? He hurried to the bathroom, looked around, and saw the footprint on the toilet lid. He climbed up and raised one of the ceiling tiles and found the cell phone. He quickly took the phone, got down, and ran back to his desk. At his desk Wayne turned on the phone and began looking through recent calls, phonebook, and text messages. There it was, all the evidence he needed against Doc, without a doubt. He went to the base radio, which was against the far wall, to call the sergeant, when Doc returned with two diet drinks.

Doc, seeing Wayne in the area of the radio and noting the startled look on his face, asked, "What's up, Wayne?"

Wayne did not answer but grabbed the microphone and yelled into it, "Sergeant, you need to ten-nineteen, nine one one." Using the ten code, Wayne thought he could get the message out without alerting Doc.

Doc, not knowing what was just said, put the drinks down, walked around behind Wayne, and unfolded the knife.

On the radio the sergeant answered, "Ten-nine?" Say again.

Doc, not waiting around to find out, lunged with the opened commando knife at Wayne, who had his back to the door. The first stab went deep into Wayne's back between the shoulder blades, and with Wayne, still trying to make contact with the sergeant on the radio, felt the pain and the blade in his back.

Wayne yelled, "Sergeant, it is the Doc."

Wayne, pushed into the wall with a knife in his back, tried to move, but Doc, being as tall and heavy as Wayne, had him pinned to the wall. Doc withdrew the blade, and blood poured out of the wound. Doc stabbed Wayne again, this time under the rib cage, still in Wayne's back. This time the leverage let up, and Wayne was able to clear himself from the wall and Doc. He stumbled but caught his balance and then fell to his knees, on purpose, though, so he could get to his ankle holster and draw his Smith and Wesson five-shot .38. As he was pulling out the gun, Doc jumped and stuck the knife in Wayne's left shoulder.

Wayne fell back, but his gun had cleared leather. He tried to locate his target and fired one round. The round did find its intended target, but gave only a flesh

THE DRUG TASK FORCE

wound to Doc's right hip. Wayne was getting dizzy from the loss of blood and pain, but he managed to get to all fours and attempt to stand up, but Doc moved around behind him. When Wayne made it to his feet, Doc came at him again and sliced the inside of Wayne's arm that held the gun. Wayne turned and dropped the gun and swung a left hand toward Doc and connected with Doc's jaw, but the punch lacked enough force to knock Doc off of him. Doc returned a punch and knocked Wayne to the ground for the last time.

Doc then went around, grabbed Wayne by the hair of his head, pulled his head back, sliced Wayne's throat, and let him fall to the floor. Doc rolled Wayne over and said, "I am truly sorry."

Wayne mouthed the words, "Fuck you."

Doc laid Wayne's head down and began to get ready to leave before anyone arrived wondering what the gunshot was about. Doc tended to his wound, retrieved the four ledger books, made a phone call, left the bullpen and dugout, and escaped into the darkness. On the radio the sergeant was still trying to get back in touch with Wayne, but no more replies came from the dugout.

Chapter 32

The sergeant and Gates in the command van rolled up to the gate at the entrance to the housing addition. A Hispanic male came out of the guardhouse and approached the van on the driver's side.

"I am here to see the Warez house; can you tell me how to get there?" asked the sergeant in a very polite manner.

"You do not belong at his house. You must leave now!" the Hispanic male said with an attitude.

"Oh, but you don't understand, Warez does not belong there. We can do this the easy way or the hard way. You decide."

The man motioned for his partner to come out and help him with the unruly American who did not understand. When both men were at his window, the sergeant showed them his badge and the barrel of his Glock. The men jumped back and tried for their weapons, but the sergeant had the drop on them. He let them have several rounds each, and they fell back and to the ground.

The sergeant looked over at Gates. "Well, I gave them a choice; I guess the hard way."

THE DRUG TASK FORCE

The team, now all together, located the stairs and made their decision of how to ascend the flight of stairs. The stairs went up and around with two landings, one halfway, and then the top.

Humphries went first, on the outside wall, and then Pablo on the inside in a staggered file, followed by Lowery, Brown, Roman, Hamms, Warren, and then Matt. After their first three steps of ten steps, from the floor of the first landing a rifle appeared and fired, just ten feet away. The first few rounds struck the outside wall and hit Humphries square in the chest. He fell back and into Lowery, who caught and stopped him from falling all the way down.

Pablo and Brown returned fire, and the rifle went back behind the wall. Through the air over the heads of the team trapped on the stairs went one more flash bang. Even before it hit the landing floor, it blew, and after the bang, Pablo, Brown, and Roman turned the corner and killed the bad guy on the landing. They headed up the last ten steps in a full charge and entered a huge open game room. A pool table, arcade games, shuffleboard, poker table, and a jukebox decorated the floor space.

Pablo secured the left, and Brown the right.

Immediately at the top on each side were hallways, likely leading to bedrooms and a bathroom. On the far wall was a fireplace with another huge TV mounted to the mantel. Three couches in a half moon lined in front of the TV, and on the other two walls were pictures and more stuffed animal heads and one door on each side. The left-side door was a half door, which meant it led to the attic, and the other door was normal size, a closet. The only lighting was from hanging bar-type lamps, three in all. From under the attic door shone a light, and there was sound, moving sounds, coming from the attic.

Brown yelled out, "Someone is in the attic trying to get to the garage."

Matt, Warren, and Hamms raced back down the stairs to the kitchen and the garage door. Roman, Brown, and Pablo cleared the rest of the upstairs quickly and then got ready to enter the attic.

Lowery stayed with Humphries on the landing and was tending to his life-threatening wounds.

Back at the attic door, Pablo was lying flat as Roman opened the door. Brown, standing above Pablo, caught a glimpse of someone going down the attic stairs. "Hamms, he is all yours. He is going down the ladder now," Brown said into the radio.

Hamms, Matt, and Warren had the garage door open and entered, when they saw a man climbing down the ladder from the attic with his back to the garage door, where the three were standing and waiting. They waited for him to get on the floor before they said anything to him.

THE DRUG TASK FORCE

Hamms, with pride in his voice, shouted, "Tulsa County Sheriff Department. Do not move. Do not even flinch until I tell you to."

The man froze for a second.

"Slowly turn around, and keep those hands high and empty."

The man turned slowly with his hands up, slowly turning halfway and then three quarters, and then he dropped his right hand and went for his waist.

The man was wearing blue jeans, boots, a cowboy shirt, and a cowboy hat, with a Sig Sauer .45 in his belt. Matt, because he had more on his mind, was the first to fire and the last to stop firing on Warez. Matt, after unloading his gun, was trying to reload when Hamms stopped him.

"It is over, Matt. You got the bastard," Hamms said softly to Matt.

Matt, without missing a beat, walked over to the dead man, who he identified as Edwardo Warez, and kicked him hard in the ribs. "Now it is over. The third fucking general is dead," Matt said.

The other man on the landing was identified as Felipe Ramerez.

After a few minutes, Humphries, who had taken several rounds that went through his bulletproof vest, closed his eyes and began to take his last breath, but Lowery whispered in his ear, "We won; we got all the bad guys."

Humphries tried to smile and mouthed the words, "Hell ,yes," then smiled again, and his body went limp.

Back in the garage, Hamms let the sergeant know that they had secured the house and the three generals were dead. The sergeant confirmed the information and reported that the guard shack was now the property of the county as well.

The time was 0340 hours

As the team members were leaving the house through the garage, they received news that something had happened back at the dugout and something was terribly wrong with Wayne and the doctor.

Pablo was the first to leave. When he went through the garage and past Warez's body, he fired one round into the corpse and sang out loud "Another One Bites the Dust". Next Lowery, Brown, Roman, Warren, and Matt as well all fired one more round. Hamms, the last to come out and the moral leader, stopped by the body and looked down at Warez and then looked up to the rest of the team members, who had stopped, turned, and waited for him. Hamms looked at his team, shrugged his shoulders, and fired one round.

They all walked slowly out into the driveway and into the cold, foggy night air and waited for the sergeant to come pick them up. Pablo lit a cigarette took a long drag, let it out, breathed a sigh of relief, looked around, and took another drag. "Walker, ol' buddy, we got them all, all these fuckers are D.R.T."

Time was 0340 hours

Chapter 33

As the sergeant and Gates were headed toward the Warez house to pick up his DTF team members, he was calling the office to get a report on what Wayne was trying to tell him about Doc. The relief he was feeling that his team had just dismantled a Mexican drug cartel in its own back yard was disappearing with every word he was hearing on his cell phone. The sergeant pulled the van over to the curb so he could concentrate on what he was hearing, not his driving.

The batting cage where Wayne's desk was, was all torn up, with shelving knocked over, paper everywhere, a bullet hole in one wall, and Wayne's bloody and beaten body. The doctor was nowhere to be found, inside the office or in the parking lot. The night shift commander stated that the closet door was open and the small key box was also open, with several car keys missing. The commander asked what vehicles were with the team, so they could figure out what vehicles, if any, were missing. The sergeant and the commander went over the list of keys and cars and figured that Doc had taken the 2008 red Chevy Impala. This car was decked out with chrome wheels, dark limo tint, and a very large stereo system. The car, a drug-dealer confiscation, was a hot car with lots of speed. The dealer was also a mechanic, and with the aftermarket engine, speed was a given. The dealer used the car only to transport dope or money back and forth to Oklahoma City.

The sergeant reached over and opened up his in car computer and logged into the tracking screen. All the DTF cars were equipped with a tracking GPS unit for undercover operations, but there was a little on/off switch. When the guys start their cars, they usually turn off the system, unless it is truly needed. They tease Pablo and tell him to have his system on, so when he gets lost they can tell him which way to go.

The tracking screen came to life with a map of the city streets, and one little red dot appeared. The little red dot was traveling south on Harvard in the 7100 block. The sergeant pulled the van back onto the lane and hurried to the Warez house. He turned the corner and saw the team standing at the opening of the garage door, and the sergeant and Gates heard a single thud then saw Hamms walking toward the rest of the team.

The sergeant pulled into the driveway, and with his window down, shouted out orders. "Everyone pile in, and do it now. I will explain on the way."

Hamms asked as he was the last to crawl into the back of the van, "On the way where, and why in such a hurry?"

THE DRUG TASK FORCE

The guys all had smiles on their faces and a few tears in their eyes, but when the sergeant gave the order, they all knew something else had gone wrong. The sergeant quickly backed up and turned around and headed for the gatehouse and began to explain the new information.

Pablo, taking this news hard, pounded his fist into the headrest of Roman's seat and spoke very loudly. "I knew it! I knew it, but I just did not have any real hard proof, just my gut instinct."

"Well, do we know where he is now?" Hamms asked, still not sure of his feelings yet.

"Looks like One Twenty-first and Yale, but the car has stopped," the sergeant said, still reading the GPS map.

Doc had stopped at a farmhouse on the far southern edge of Tulsa County. The house was a drug house, but it also had money, guns, and two more men inside. Doc loaded the Impala with the two men, weapons, and cash. He knew that he had a head start, but that the team would soon be on his trail. He knew they would figure out which car he had taken and would be calling every agency to be on the lookout, so he had to get to Henryetta before they could close in on him. There he could meet more of his family and change vehicles and get into Texas and then Mexico before they could figure out which way he was headed.

"We need to figure out where he is going and fast, before he gets out of range of our computer and GPS," the sergeant stated, asking for any other ideas.

Hamms explained his train of thought to the sergeant and the rest of the team. "Call the office and have someone look at those maps from the warehouse. He will travel that route so he can meet with his people along the way,"

The sergeant drove the guys to their cars, where they bailed out and then jumped into their own vehicles and started south.

In the car, Hamms was worried that the sergeant would call for backup and other agencies to help. Not that he would not appreciate their help, but he wanted his team to finish this, and he did not care how they finished it, so he had to say something. "Sergeant, can we keep this to ourselves, at least until we have lost him?"

"I never once thought of asking for help," the sergeant replied.

"Thank you," Hamms replied on the radio and then grinned from ear to ear.

The guys in three cars had only reached 51st Street and Highway 75 when the sergeant told them the Impala was moving again. The sergeant's cell phone rang, and the commander told him that the next stop for Doc looked to be south of Henryetta on old Highway 75. The sergeant relayed the information

THE DRUG TASK FORCE

to the team members, and they decided to stop for gas at 111th at the Gas-N-Go station. Hamms walked over to the van and asked the sergeant, "What is after Henryetta?"

The sergeant replied as he was looking at a map, "We have to stop him there, because that is where he will change cars and take any of the three highways south. After Henryetta, we will have to call for help. We cannot cover three highways looking for an unidentified make and model vehicle."

"Well, I guess we better step on it and get there," Hamms said as he took the gas nozzle out of his car.

Pablo came out of the store with a thermos of coffee and a box of fresh doughnuts. Pablo, looking at everyone who was staring at him, said with a big smile, "Really, I paid for the doughnuts. They gave me the thermos and the coffee, though not as good as my favorite cafe, The Crescent Cafe."

After they divided up the doughnuts, the four-vehicle parade hit the highway southbound, not sparing any miles per hour.

The sergeant, on the radio again, relayed information to all. "Computer is going down, but the red dot is still going south about twenty miles ahead of us. We need to close in, but not catch up until he is in town."

Time was 0412 hours

Highway 75 was a nice smooth four-lane road with

two lanes north and two lanes south with a wide grassy median. There were no lights on the highway. The only light was provided by the vehicles and the moon, this night a full moon, but hidden by the low, dark, rain-filled clouds and a dense fog that at low spots brought visibility down to half a football field or even shorter in some areas. At that time of the morning, the traffic was light, and most of it was headed north into Tulsa. The cars took up both lanes, with Pablo on the left and the sergeant in the right lane and the other two close behind.

The terrain was long hills up and down and through the wooded country of East Central Oklahoma. No billboards, and only a few closed convenience stores along the highway; other than that, there was nothing to look at except the white lines and all the deer-crossing caution signs.

After Doc had finished off Wayne, he found the car keys, left the office, and drove a red Impala straight to another location within the cartel network. He picked up his supplies and two other young Hispanic males and headed to Henryetta. There he would change cars, freshen up, and head on toward Texas and then the border. Once on the highway southbound, Doc slowed down for the weather and to avoid any Oklahoma highway patrols in the area. To his new two best friends, he explained what was happening and who was chasing them.

THE DRUG TASK FORCE

Doc explained the plan to the two new guys. "Once we get to the house, Juan, you get out at the gate and keep an eye out. Hopefully they will not be too close behind us. The deputies will be in trucks and a white van, or any other combination of those four vehicles, you call me."

They had just passed the Beggs exit and were about thirty minutes from Henryetta.

"Raul, you will stay with me, and we will load the other car. We need to be back on the road in half an hour or so."

Just to the south of the Beggs exit, the road sloped downward and the fog was so thick that Doc slowed his escape to twenty-five and thirty miles per hour. The terrain was hilly, up and down, and in the middle of nowhere with nothing except rabbits, coyotes, and deer. Just as Doc was driving upward on the second hill, seven deer came across the road in front of the Impala. Doc, going slow, was able to avoid the string of deer, but not without sliding two wheels off the road. He regained control, cussed, and then proceeded south.

The farther out of town the team drove, the thicker the fog became, and the speed of their pursuit slowed. They were driving sixty to sixty-five miles an hour with their fingers crossed on a wing and a prayer, just trying to make up time and distance.

Hamms got on the radio just to break the silence and asked, "Someone better come up with something. I am getting crossed eyed, and I am not used to driving like Pablo."

Pablo tried to reply, but with a mouth full of doughnut, all he could do was choke, laugh, and spit food everywhere.

The sergeant answered, "How about an update? We are still gaining ground, looks like about ten or twelve miles behind. We still don't want to get too close too soon."

Hamms, speaking in the silence to his team, said, "Boys, I just want you to know that this team is the best I have ever been associated with, and I am proud to know each and every one of you. With the loss of some of our own today, I want us to remember them and honor them with respect and love. We need to finish this, one way or the other, but Doc dies tonight."

Lowery answered quickly, "It ain't gonna be the other way, and we ain't dyin' tonight, boys."

They just drove past the Beggs exit and were on a downhill slope of the highway, which meant that the fog was even thicker. The sergeant's van swerved to the right quickly, and Pablo's truck braked hard, as another string of deer was crossing the highway, but the team was driving too fast. The van swerved right and then back to the left as it left the shoulder and went into the grass. As it came back onto the blacktop, the sergeant was still trying to regain control of the van as it slid sideways down the highway. Still in the right lane, the sergeant was turning the wheel trying to get the van headed in the right direction, and the van tipped and did a barrel roll down the highway. The roll started on the passenger side, then the roof, driver's side, wheels, all four sides, and one more time before the vehicle came to rest on its top just off the roadway. The wheels were still turning and the engine was running and a few moans and groans came from inside, the only other sounds in the night.

Pablo, being a country boy who had driven the country roads all his life, was trained for just this situation. As a father, Pablo taught his kids when driving the back roads and something jumped in front of you, just keep going straight, brake, but do not swerve. It will be easier to fix your car than your body. When the deer magically appeared in the highway, Pablo hit the brakes but kept his truck straight. The truck tried to swerve to the right, but Pablo released the brake, the tires caught hold, and the truck straightened up again.

Warren, sitting in the front seat, shouted as he watched the sergeant and his van tumble and come to rest.

Hamms, who was following behind the van, had plenty of time to slow and stop behind the crashed van. He exited the truck and ran to the van.

RUSTY POPE

Pablo's truck ran into the last deer in the line, and when Pablo got his truck stopped and off the highway, the deer's tail was stuck in the grill and a headlight dangled from where it should have been.

Lowery, in the last car, was able to avoid all the debris from the crash and the deer. He pulled to a stop behind and beside Hamms's truck.

Hamms and Roman were the first to reach the van, which was smoking and hissing and smelling like burnt rubber, antifreeze, and burning electrical equipment. Roman and Hamms both went to the back doors and ripped them open. Hamms went inside, as Lowery and Brown arrived. Lowery had a fire extinguisher and went to work on the undercarriage of the van. Brown went in the van with Hamms, looking for the sergeant and Gates. Both the deputies had to move several things around to reach the cab. Roman climbed up on the van and found the sergeant hanging in the front seat by his seatbelt.

"Hamms, Brown, you guys find Gates yet?" Roman shouted at the other two deputies.

"Not yet! We have not made it to the front," Brown answered as he threw another box out the back doors.

"I got Sergeant. He is bleeding but breathing," Roman shouted even louder, now that the motor was making more racket than it did when the crash first happened.

THE DRUG TASK FORCE

Hamms finally reached the front of the van and moved some equipment around and found Bates, who was unconscious, but also breathing. Pablo, Warren and Matt reached the van, and Pablo had already called the office and requested an ambulance. The van's main function for the team was for when they have to deal with meth labs. The back of the van had wooden shelving built into the back, for the team's self-contained breathing apparatus tanks, chemical suits and masks, evidence buckets and many more supplies. When the van rolled some of the cabinets came open and the contents went everywhere. It appeared that Gates was hit in the back of the head by some of the buckets, a folding chair, and other items. The back of Gates' head was gashed open and bleeding, and also blood oozed from his nose and right ear. The blood from his ear concerned Hamms the most, but with further inspection, he saw that the bleeding was from his ear was because it was nearly cut off. When the van rolled, Gates' right side hit his window hard enough to shatter the window and his ear.

Hamms and Brown cut the belt, released Gates, and dragged him out the back of the van, and tended to his wounds. Roman and Matt were on top of the van and could not get the crushed door to open, so they decided to pull the sergeant through the window. They figured it would be easier to pull him up than to cut him loose and try to catch him.

Pablo got inside the van and held the sergeant steady until they got a good grip and were ready to pull him out.

"Okay, Pablo, we got him. Now cut the belt," Roman announced to Pablo.

Pablo cut the belt, and all the weight fell onto Pablo's shoulders, but just for a second. Roman and Matt began to pull, and Pablo helped guide the sergeant out of the window. Once they got him through the window, they checked for serious injuries. The worst they found was the sergeant's left arm was broken, a compound fracture, which meant part of his bone was sticking through the skin. They applied a makeshift bandage to the arm and moved him to the edge, where Warren and Lowery were waiting. They lowered the sergeant off the side of the van to the two others, who carefully carried the sergeant away from the van. With the demolished van and Pablo's damaged truck and two seriously injured team members, a critical decision had to be made and made quickly.

Hamms, sensing desperate looks on the faces of his team, took charge and ordered, "Right now it is oh four forty-five hours, and we have lost some serious time and distance, if we want to catch Doc."

Roman added his two cents. "We need to make a move!"

THE DRUG TASK FORCE

Hamms continued, "Matt and Warren are going to stay here with our injured, in Pablo's truck, and wait for the ambulance. The rest of us will load up in my truck and Lowery's car and get started. Once the ambulance picks up the sergeant and Gates, you guys head south and let us know, and we will give you the directions."

Pablo jumped in with Lowery and Brown, with Hamms and Roman in his truck, and once again the team headed south.

Once they were back on the road, Hamms called Brown on the cell phone.

Hamms, still in the zone, said, "I have an idea about how to get a GPS on the Impala. If you call the office and get the tracker code, you can dial it in your iPhone and receive signals," he stated to the other techno-geek, Brown.

"I think you are right, because that is how we plugged it into our mobile computer. I will get on it right now," Brown answered and went right to work.

After five minutes on the phone with the sheriff's office, Brown dialed the code into his phone and hit the Send button. After just a few seconds, a map appeared and a little red flashing light came on. The light was just outside of Henryetta.

"Hamms, I got him. He is just now at the Henryetta exit, so we have not lost as much time as we thought.

We are fifteen minutes behind him right now," Brown informed Hamms as well as the rest of the team.

"How's your vision up front?" Hamms asked, as he was even more worried than before about the driving conditions.

"Lowery says it is good, so we are going to pick it up a little."

"Hey, everyone, I just got word the ambulance just arrived. The other two will be en route in maybe ten minutes."

Doc and his two passengers, Juan and Raul, took the exit off Highway 75 and turned east onto New Park Road. The low-fuel light turned on, and Doc hoped that the car could go six more miles before it ran out of gas. Once on New Park Road, they left town to the east and followed the road to the Oknoname Reservoir exit and pulled down a long dirt driveway to a well- fortified farmhouse. The car sputtered and stopped just outside the mechanical gate, and the only problem was that the drive was one lane and a 200-yard hike to the house.

Doc told the new boys, "We will leave everything in the car for now and unload it when we get back here and then head for the border."

Juan, a twenty-something Hispanic male, was a new member of the family. He had been recruited at the end of the summer, and this was the first time he

THE DRUG TASK FORCE

had ever been in the U.S. Raul was in his thirties and had been with the Warez Cartel since it was formed. In fact he was part of the enforcers and had many kills under his belt.

They opened the gate and took only a few items with them before they started for the farmhouse. Doc was trying to hurry, but he did not expect the team to be closing in on him this fast.

Their tracking device was worth its weight in gold as the team began to see the lights of the major highway intersections on the north side of Henryetta.

"Okay, the light has gone off, so the car engine is turned off. We need to exit, go under the highway, and look for a left turn onto New Park Road. We will follow it around to a pond, and it looks like a long one-lane driveway." Brown was now giving direction to all.

Roman had been quiet since the reload after the crash, but he had been looking in his cell phone phonebook, looking for the number of an Okmulgee County Task Force deputy that he had worked with several times in the past. Roman came up with his own plans and shared them. "Here it is a number for Sean Grant. He is on the drug team for Okmulgee County. I can call him and tell him we are here, just so he knows and he knows why."

"Go ahead and make the call. Someone ought to know the shit is about to hit the fan," Hamms replied.

RUSTY POPE

Roman let the phone ring and ring and ring until a groggy male voice answered, "This better be important."

"Oh it is. Wake the fuck up and listen up; I've got a job for you." Roman had to explain twice who he was and how the two knew each other. After that, Roman explained what had happened and what was about to happen.

Grant gave Roman some information about the house and what to expect. Grant had been to the house several times for recreation, not business.

Roman hung up the phone and told Hamms what Grant had told him. "I just hope Grant is still trustworthy," Roman whispered more to himself than anyone else.

Grant was still a good guy, for he got up and dressed and was in his car within ten minutes of the call, and he did not contact anyone else.

Time was 0520 hours

Lowery found New Park Road. "Here is the drive, and it is one lane," Lowery announced as he turned east and led the cars onto the drive.

Hamms followed as they drove toward the last escaping members of the Warez Cartel. "Let's stop here, get ready, then drive in blacked out," Hamms ordered.

"Damn, I wish I had had one more cup of coffee before those damn deer spilled it all," Pablo complained as he got out of the car and began to load up.

THE DRUG TASK FORCE

As the Warez trio reached the front yard of the farmhouse, there were ten cars and trucks parked in the yard and in front of the garage. The farmhouse was built in the 1940s, and it looked just like a Norman Rockwell farmhouse, a wooden, two-story frame structure with a big chimney and front porch and lots of windows to let in the light and help cool the house in the hot summer months. The only new renovation was the roof. It was a light brown metal roof that looked just as authentic as if it were the original roof. The lawn needed to be cut one more time before the fall arrived, because the grass was shin high and very thick.

When the three men got into the yard, the motion-detector lights came on, and two pit bulls growled and barked as they came out of their dog houses as far as their chains would them. Light shone through the front-room windows, but as Doc opened the front door, only the stereo was making noise. The music was low, and there were people everywhere in various stages of dress and drunkenness. In the far corner of the large living room in a recliner was a naked man and young woman sleeping, while just to their right on the couch was a petite young female giving a young Hispanic male a blow job. In the middle of the floor was another passed-out naked couple, with another couple right next to them doing it doggy style.

RUSTY POPE

On the coffee table that was pushed to one side was white powder spilled everywhere and marijuana joints in all different sizes and shapes and a few bongs and glass pipes. Out of the kitchen and into the living room came a twenty- something Hispanic female wearing only red thong panties and sporting a very nice set of pierced boobs. She was surprised by the new guest and let out a scream that could wake the dead. The scream was so loud and terrifying that the doggy-style couple stopped in mid stroke. The man dove off of the woman and tried to get to his feet and to a shotgun in the opposite corner of the room. The young man getting a slow blow job jumped, rolled off the sofa, and was digging under the couch for his handgun.

Doc started yelling at everyone in Spanish and got everyone's attention. He ordered all the men to get dressed, armed, and outside and to shoot anyone who showed up. Doc and Raul went upstairs to gather some items, and Juan went to the garage to get their getaway car ready.

Juan, not nearly as excited about leaving as he was excited about all the naked women in the house, went through the dining room toward the garage door. He grabbed the girl with the pierced nipples by the arm and made her go to the garage with him. In all, five Hispanic drunk and hung over males dressed, armed themselves, and went outside to look for any intruders.

THE DRUG TASK FORCE

Once upstairs in the master bedroom, Doc went to a hidden safe in a false wall in the closet and turned the dial right, left, right, left, and then opened the safe. Raul handed Doc one empty suitcase, and Doc filled it with money and other important documents. Raul took another empty suitcase and filled it with handguns and ammunition. Before they left the bedroom, both men grabbed AK-47s, locked and loaded them, and loaded extra magazines in their back pockets. On their way back down the stairs, they heard the pit bulls barking and then could tell that the barking and growling was running away from the house.

Just as the team was parking and getting ready for the assault, Hamms got a call from Matt, who said the ambulance had left and he was on his way. Hamms gave him the directions to the house and the information that he might run into Sean Grant, a task force member from Okmulgee.

The team drove the one-lane road blacked out until it came to the red Impala and the open gate. They parked in a manner that would prevent anyone from leaving the farmhouse by way of the driveway, and also disabled the car. They put on their night-vision goggles and made their way through the gate and toward the house. They could hear some dogs barking in the background.

RUSTY POPE

Roman said he hoped they were not pit bulls and headed their way.

The five Hispanic males, once outside the house in the cold morning air, were starting to sober up some. Two of the men went to the pits, unchained them, and let them go. The pits, once they were freed, took off running to the drive and then disappeared in the darkness toward the gate. Once out of sight, the dogs quit barking and playing and began to hunt for intruders.

Grant had told Roman about the house and the land it was on. He said the drive was not wired, but the woods had several traps, the kind with claws that shut when stepped in, so the best method of approach was straight in on the driveway. The team members did not like being that much in the open, so they walked in the ditches just off the drive.

The time was 0535 hours and was the last time they heard the dogs barking. They then began their approach to the house. Brown led on the right, followed by Lowery, ten yards back. Pablo led on the left, with Roman and Hamms following, equally spaced. The night was cold and dark, for the moon was still hidden behind a dark blanket of clouds. A light north wind helped cover the noise made by the team traveling in leaf-filled ditches along the drive. The rain showers in Oklahoma had come and gone, leaving the leaves and grass wet and quiet.

THE DRUG TASK FORCE

Brown looked at Pablo and got his attention and asked him if he heard the barking. Pablo could not hear the dogs anymore either, which was unsettling to the leaders. With their night vision, the darkness was working in their favor, because they could see in low or no light. Brown raised clinched fist into the air to signal the rest of the team to halt and listen. "Anyone else hear something running?" asked Brown.

"I do and it sounds like it is getting closer," Pablo whispered.

As Pablo finished his sentence, he dropped to one knee, and Brown did the same. Just ten yards ahead, the driveway curved, and from the curve came two dogs running full bore at the team. Through the goggles the targets were green and not very clear, but the men could tell they were no lap dogs. With their Glocks still supporting suppressors, Brown and Pablo opened fire on the attacking dogs. The other three men also went to one knee and were ready to help the two leaders if they needed it. The dogs, charging at full speed, were on top of Brown and Pablo within seconds after they made the curve. Brown fired first and repeatedly, trying to hit a fast-charging target. After five rounds, he hit his dog just as it lunged at him. The dog took two to the chest and landed in Brown's lap. Brown had fallen backwards when the dog jumped.

RUSTY POPE

Pablo started firing just after Brown but missed, and the lunging dog knocked Pablo off his feet and onto his back. The dog fell off to the side and was getting ready to eat Pablo. Roman got a clean shot and finished off the attack with two shots.

"Thanks, Roman. I guess I need to practice with these goggles."

"No problem. I shoot the neighbor's cat while wearing these goggles all the time."

"I hope our misses don't warn the others we are here," Brown whispered to Pablo.

After the dogs took off, the five men began to move up the drive and through the woods. Since they lived at the house, they knew where the traps and flares were placed throughout the woods, so they were moving through the woods watching and listening for anything traveling down the drive. Just before they reached the halfway mark, they heard several thuds and even some whistling noises through the trees. They also heard what sounded like a couple of dog whimper and then nothing. Now they were even more ready, but without being able to see, they were still at a disadvantage, so they stopped and took up defensive positions just twenty yards short of the big curve.

With the night-vision goggles, the men could see shapes and see movement and anything that created some heat would show up green. As the team made the curve, Brown once again raised his clinched fist, and the rest dropped to a knee.

"I have one bad guy on Pablo's side of the drive beside a tree," Brown whispered to all.

"Brown one is fifteen yards in front, a little left on our side. Oh no, he is peeing," Lowery also said in a whisper.

One of the Hispanic men just could not stand or hold it any longer, and thinking no one was in the woods, stopped and took a pee.

"Okay that's two. Anymore?" Hamms asked, keeping track.

"I see them. There are three in the middle of the road. Roman, Hamms, move up here on my right and get a line of sight," Pablo announced.

Pablo, Roman, and Hamms all got on their targets, and Brown and Lowery covered theirs.

"Everyone got a shot?"

All answered.

"On three, drop 'em. One, two, three," Hamms stated.

As soon as the men heard "Three," they all fired twice, and five men fell dead right where they were standing. One man had a finger on the trigger, so when he was hit twice, he pulled the trigger, and fourteen rounds fired and echoed through the woods.

"Damn it! Who keeps their finger on the trigger?" Roman angrily shouted into the darkness.

RUSTY POPE

"Well, there goes our surprise attack," Hamms said as he looked completely dejected.

"Just wonder how many more before we get to the house," Lowery complained to Brown as they reloaded.

"I think it's time for *Shock and Awe Five*. I will lead, you guys on each flank and in a wedge and shoot any and everything. Time to go." Pablo roared to life and on a mission.

Doc and Raul, having carried the two completely full suitcases downstairs and to the dining room, went into the kitchen and fixed themselves some sandwiches. They were still not rushing, but they were not wasting time either.

"Amanda, come here. I need some help," Doc ordered feeling pretty good about himself.

Amanda, the petite young girl that was busy with the doggy style came over to Doc and began to rub and caress his crotch.

Raul, seeing an opportunity, went back into the living to wake the woman in the recliner. Raul grabbed the girl by the hair, dragged her off the recliner, and then helped her up and onto the couch. He dropped his pants and began to do the girl from behind as she slumped over the arm of the couch.

Doc, while eating his sandwich, was getting a deep-throat blow job.

THE DRUG TASK FORCE

Juan had already finished with his nipple-pierced beauty, and while opening the garage door, heard gunfire coming from up the drive. He ran through the door that opened up into the dining room and saw the doctor getting oral pleasure.

Juan, in a panic, yelled out to Doc, "Sir, gunfire outside, and it sounded like one of our guns."

Doc threw his sandwich down, pushed the girl off his business, and yelled for Raul to get ready. They carried the suitcases out and loaded them into a black 2011 Jeep Cherokee. The three men ran back inside, grabbed their guns, and were back in the garage when they noticed the motion-sensor lights switch on. Juan ran to the big door and took a position just inside the garage door.

Doc, shaking his head in disbelief, said to himself, "Damn, these guys are good."

The guys were marching right down the middle of the drive with Pablo leading, Roman and Hamms flanking his right, and Brown and Lowery on his left. They made their way to one more slight curve without any resistance, and the area opened up into a front yard and house. They saw a picturesque farmhouse with a yard and driveway full of trucks and cars. The garage door was open and well lit, and after just a couple of more steps, the motion-detector lights came on. The men removed their goggles and hid behind some of the cars while their eyes adjusted.

Pablo, seeing into the garage, shouted, "Movement in the garage. They know we are here."

"Boys, it is time to go to work," Brown proclaimed to the team with confidence.

"Doc's got some serious shit breathing down on him now," Lowery blurted as he moved to the front door.

Pablo and Roman and Hamms worked their way closer to the opening of the garage using the cars for cover and concealment, while Brown and Lowery continued to move left, more toward the front door.

Roman pointed to the left front corner of the garage and made hand signals to the others.

When the lights came on, Juan ran to a corner of the garage to wait, and Doc told Raul to get back in the house and watch the front door.

Doc went back to the dining room and gathered up the four women who were now fully clothed and very scared. None of the women were accustomed to having sex, drugs, and people shooting guns at them all in the same night. Doc calmed them down and then told them to load up in the Jeep. Doc was hoping that the deputies would think that the car leaving the garage was him, and attack the car. When they were shooting at the car, it would give him and his two other men good shots. He gave Amanda the key and had the women crawl out of sight to the car and get in and fire it

THE DRUG TASK FORCE

up. He said he would give her a signal to take off, but he did not tell her he was hoping the deputies would shoot at her. With Raul covering the front door and Juan in the garage, he was ready to execute his plan.

Pablo, Roman, and Hamms, all behind different cars, had good vision into the garage, but neither of the three could see the interior door.

Brown and Lowery had made it to the front porch when they noticed a Hispanic male, not Doc, guarding and watching the front door. The screen door was an old fashioned wooden screen door with no glass. If they could make it onto the porch, they could get close enough to the door to take out the sentry without much risk.

Doc gave Amanda the signal to drive. She started the Jeep, put it into drive, and started out. She was so scared that she started slowly. Juan was not in on the plan, so he panicked when the Jeep started to drive out of the garage. He stepped out toward the Jeep, three thuds sounded off, and the young man took one more step and fell to the ground without ever knowing what happened.

Amanda, having seen Juan get shot, panicked and stomped on the gas, and the Jeep roared to life and almost jumped out of the garage. She lost control, let go of the steering wheel to cover her face, and drove into the first two cars that were parked closest to the garage door. Roman dove to the right and Pablo to the left. When Pablo dove left, Amanda's Jeep hit one of the other cars, turned right, and caught Pablo in mid dive. The front of the Jeep ran squarely into a second car, caught Pablo's leg, and pinned him between the two.

Pablo cried out in pain as Hamms approached the passenger side of the car. When he could see inside, he noticed four scared and unarmed girls, but no Doc. The sound of an AK then took over the night as the bullets ripped through the Jeep, heading toward Hamms. He fell, un-hit, to the ground and rolled out of sight. Roman, using the Jeep as a shield, broke the driver's window, reached in, and put the Jeep into reverse, releasing Pablo's pinned leg and allowing him to take cover. Roman followed the Jeep back into the garage, all the while Amanda was crying, screaming, and punching at him. Roman threw the Jeep into park and with one quick move, hit Amanda on the side of the head and knocked her out cold.

Hamms started firing into the garage toward the interior door to force the rifle to retreat, and it worked. The AK went silent.

Brown and Lowery were on the porch by then with one on each side of the door, and neither one could see far enough inside the entryway. Lowery, with a big window behind him, signaled to Brown that

THE DRUG TASK FORCE

he was going to flash bang the window, and give him time to take the front door. Lowery crawled up past the big window and readied the bang, gave Brown the heads up, broke the window, and threw the bang. The familiar bright light flashed, followed by the bang, and Brown entered the screen door into the living room, searching for the one who was guarding the door, but no one was there.

Lowery followed behind, and the two made their way halfway into the room, when from behind the wooden door, a man stepped out and cut loose with his AK. Both dove for cover, but Lowery was late and took one round to the back of his upper left leg.

Brown had made it behind a loveseat but did not stop moving and came out the other side, throwing lead toward the direction of the rifle.

Lowery had been hit, but not stopped, for he too rolled beside a desk and returned fire. Raul, who had the element of surprise but not the experience to sustain the attack, was hit repeatedly, and his AK went silent as so went his life.

Roman and Hamms secured the garage and were listening to the battle coming from inside the house.

After the gunfire stopped, Roman yelled into the radio, "Brown, Lowery, you guys good?"

Brown quickly answered, "Lowery's hit, but living room secured."

"Pablo has a broken leg, garage secured," Hamms relayed.

Hamms moved up to the inside door and yelled, "Doc, you mother fucker, come out where we can see you and your hands." Hamms made the announcement, not sure why.

Silence was the only answer.

Hamms and Roman entered the dining room. Brown, helping the bleeding Lowery, also entered the dining room, and they met up. The three men hurried back into the living room and were about to climb the stairs when they heard Pablo on the radio.

Doc, being surrounded, needed a place to hide, so just inside the garage door; he slipped into a cupboard and closed the door. He could hear two men enter into the dining room and then the kitchen, so he decided to move. He slipped out the garage door and back into the garage and was on his way out.

"Boys, he is in the garage. Hurry!" Pablo whispered into his radio.

When Pablo was caught between the two cars, he had lost his Glock, and it was just out of reach, so when Doc noticed him lying on the driveway ground, he was unarmed and an easy target. Pablo had already gotten out his "dull ass" pocketknife, unfolded it, and was ready.

THE DRUG TASK FORCE

"Well, Pablo, I guess you are the lucky bastard that I get to kill today, and you are the one I really wanted to fuck up," Doc exclaimed as he approached.

Pablo, thinking now was the time, quickly rolled over and threw his knife. Just as Pablo was rolling the team burst into the garage and opened up on Doc. Pablo's knife stuck in Doc's belly, certainly not a lethal wound, but it stuck. Doc took many rounds in the back, stumbled forward, and fell beside Pablo. Pablo crawled over and whispered in his dying ear, "And another one gone." Pablo sang to the dying man.

Doc rolled his head toward Pablo and tried to say something, when Pablo poked him in the eye.

"Pablo, is this son of a bitch bothering you?" Hamms said, grinning as he walked toward Doc.

"Yes, can you do something about it?"

Hamms walked over and stood above Doc.

"Don't ever mess with the DTF. Now get out of my country!" Hamms almost choked with delight.

Hamms stuck his Glock barrel to Doc's chest and heart and fired. Doc closed his good eye for the last time.

After the final shot, Hamms and Brown were busy with Lowery's bleeding leg. They put a tourniquet on the leg and plugged the hole with bandages. Roman stayed with Pablo and used two broom handles to tie a splint on his leg. Matt, Warren, and Grant arrived, followed by an ambulance that loaded and transported Lowery and Pablo back to Tulsa.

Before Karen got to the hospital to meet Pablo, he was busy getting ready for his wife. He had one of the nurses give him a clean shave with just his usual mustache, and he left a little of the sideburns. He could not talk any of the nurses into a haircut, but they did clean him up a little. When he rolled out of the room, Karen was waiting for him, and he could tell she got his last message, the one from Sonny. It was a nice reunion, a real nice reunion. They embraced, and Sonny whispered into her ear, "One more year." Karen leaned back, looked into the eyes of her husband, and could tell he meant it. She smiled, and they hugged longer and tighter than they had in many months.

In all the raids, the collected evidence netted fourteen vehicles, twenty pounds shy of a ton of weed, 113 kilos of ice, and 3.2 million dollars in U.S. currency, just from the Tulsa area. The Feds finished the roundup of other cartel evidence in Oklahoma and the supply route from Mexico to Chicago. In Oklahoma alone, sixty-eight illegals were deported back to Mexico, including the four females from the farmhouse.

Marlin Organ returned to duty after two days of rest. Johnny Walker was released from the hospital for two reasons: he was healed from his wounds, and the young nurses were complaining, so after four weeks,

THE DRUG TASK FORCE

he was released and rejoined the DTF after they were reinstated six weeks later.

Dan Workman did not lose his arm but did lose the use of it, so he retired from the ATF and joined the task force as the new criminal analyst.

Lowery and Pablo both rehabbed their legs and were released from doctor's care in mid-January.

The internal investigation of the DTF took three months, and all team members were cleared of any wrongdoing. There was some question as to the number of rounds Warez took, but the men were cleared and started back to work in March. They received numerous awards, but without any fanfare or publicity, because they worked under cover.

The funerals for the fallen law enforcement deputies were respectful, memorable, and honorable events for the families and the sheriff's office, for law enforcement agencies from all over Oklahoma and even the country were represented.

The team planned a trip to Colorado to Gates' house for a little R and R in the mountains at the end of July.

Don't miss it.

THE END